The Siege

Tales from a Revolution: Virginia

Also by Lars D. H. Hedbor,
available from Brief Candle Press:

The Prize: Tales From a Revolution - Vermont
The Light: Tales From a Revolution - New-Jersey
The Smoke: Tales From a Revolution - New-York
The Declaration: Tales From a Revolution - South-Carolina
The Break: Tales From a Revolution - Nova-Scotia
The Wind: Tales From a Revolution - West-Florida
The Darkness: Tales From a Revolution - Maine
The Path: Tales From a Revolution - Rhode-Island
The Freedman: Tales From a Revolution - North-Carolina
The Tree: Tales From a Revolution - New-Hampshire
The Mine: Tales From a Revolution - Connecticut
The Will: Tales From a Revolution - Pennsylvania
The Convention: Tales From a Revolution - Massachusetts
The Oath: Tales From a Revolution - Georgia
The Powder: Tales From a Revolution - Bermuda

The Siege

Lars D. H. Hedbor

Brief Candle
Press

Cover and book design: Brief Candle Press.
Cover image based on "Bavarian Landscape," Albert Bierstadt, 1850.
Map reproduction courtesy of Library of Congress, Geography and Map Division.
Fonts: Allegheney, Doves Type, and IM FELL English.

First Brief Candle Press edition published 2020.
www.briefcandlepress.com

ISBN: 978-1-942319-41-2

Dedication

*To the many defenders of liberty
who have sacrificed of their own bodies
for the preservation of freedom*

Chapter I

Nathaniel Wooster never saw which of the advancing Redcoats fired the shot that hit him. The line of enemy horsemen had come close enough to become individual men with distinct features, expressions, and even voices before his commander had given the shouted order to fire.

Just after his musket roared in his ear and kicked back into his shoulder, Nathaniel felt as though he'd been punched hard on the arm that supported the wooden stock. The sensation honestly confused him at first, until he realized that his hand would no longer hold the weight of his weapon. He watched the precious musket tumble to the ground from his suddenly insensate fingers even as his knees began to feel weak.

Before he'd even had time to register the pain of the wound, however, the British line was on them, sabers flashing among the hapless American militiamen who still stood. Though they'd been drilled and trained to regard themselves as soldiers, most of them were hardly more than farmers or tradesmen, and none of them had any sense of how to defend themselves against a yard of brilliant, biting steel, descending to slice and tear flesh.

As he lay on the ground, his musket forgotten in the mud nearby, Nathaniel had just sufficient presence of mind to perceive that he was one of the lucky ones. The man who'd earlier stood to his left now lay on his back, eyes unblinking to the sky, his neck sliced so deeply that Nathaniel could see the white of bone inside the sagging wound. The man on his right was moaning and clutching at his belly, where the passage of a British saber had sliced through cloth, skin, and guts with equal indifference. Though Nathaniel had seen little action before now, he had no doubt that this would be that man's last day on Earth.

The redcoat footsoldiers who'd followed the cavalry charge were now pushing and shoving amongst the few Americans who still stood, using their muskets as clubs, and the horsemen wheeled about through the massed Americans, swinging their now-befouled sabers in clear menace as they strove with their enemies. Nathaniel heard a grunt behind him, and a British soldier fell facing him, clutching at his chest. The man's eyes locked onto his, and for the space of a few lazy heartbeats—heard as a rush in Nathaniel's ears, and seen as a rhythmic surge of blood between the other man's fingers—they stared at each other.

Then the other man's eyes rolled back into his head, and he was still—aside from the slowing trickle of blood into the bare earth beneath him. Soon enough, even that ceased, and Nathaniel willed himself to look away.

After what seemed like an eternity of slowing, sporadic gunfire in the distance and the screams and moans of men nearby and further strewn about the field, Nathaniel heard the cry passed from voice to voice.

"Quarter! They've asked quarter! The day is ours!"

As he focused on his labored breathing, Nathaniel idly wondered whether the white flag would be honored this time, or whether someone would again violate it and precipitate another round of senseless violence. His thoughts were tending to wander now, though, and he could not seem to hold onto a single thread for very long.

His thoughts focused on the awful question of whether he would see his Ma again, or watch another sunrise from the top of the bluff back home. He had often enough paused in his morning chores to enjoy the sight that it was graven in his mind. He recalled how the purpling horizon gave way to deeper reds than even that which now seeped through his enemy's fingers, finally punctuated by a sudden gasp of brilliant sunlight as the day began.

How would this day end? Would he sink into a grateful slumber, or would he find a more lengthy rest in an anonymous grave, accompanied by friends and enemies alike? Would he be reunited with his brother, who had been carried off by the pox so many years before, and would they play their favorite games with hoop and stick in some celestial field?

Or would he lay here in this field of carnage, drifting in and out of the world of pain and fear, unrelieved by any sleep, whether eternal or just that of an ordinary night?

His stomach lurched at the thought of his Ma left questioning for month after month about his fate, or worse yet, receiving certain word by an impersonal post that her only remaining son would never return.

He was just picturing this dismal possibility in cruel detail when he heard a squad moving over the field, and a voice calling out, "Here's one that's still breathing, Lieutenant." A boot appeared before his eyes, and Nathaniel wondered at it, struck by the lack of splashed grime on its well-blacked, supple leather.

The man bent and not ungently rolled Nathaniel over to lie on his back. The movement sparked agonies in his arm, and he cried out as the world closed in around him in gathering darkness. He could see, though, that the man's elegantly appointed jacket was crimson, and his expression disdainful.

"Bring a litter over here. Our orders are to treat all wounded, regardless of whether they be ours or theirs."

Orders were called out and answered, and Nathaniel was aware of being lifted and moved, the ground falling away beneath him, and the churned earth of the battlefield falling behind him. He noticed the scent of gunpowder, primarily by the fact that it was now fading as they moved away from the scene of the discharges.

As the British soldiers at his head and foot carried him along, they stumbled and jostled him from time to time, each jolt of movement costing him a fresh jolt of pain. He found himself wishing that he could pass into the blessed relief of unconsciousness, so that he might miss the experience of feeling blood cooling and stiffening under his sleeve, as well as the pain. It ranged from a constant ache to the sharp agony of each bit of motion he felt.

Pain became a companion along the way toward whatever destination his saviors—or captors?—bore him, unwelcome but dependable. Beyond the pain of his arm, he could feel a dull ache in his belly, and it occurred to him to worry whether he'd been injured there as well. Had one of the flashing sabers sliced into him unnoticed, leaving him alike with his companion on the line, his guts spilling out onto the field?

Or was it, perhaps, just the old familiar sensation of unrequited hunger, common enough in these past months? His head ached, too, and he was struck by the thought that it might be more profitable to consider what parts of his being were not in pain.

His feet were, for a mercy, not on the ground, not carrying him over mile after weary mile toward an uncertain fate. His toes itched from never having been completely dry for these many months, but he wouldn't call that pain, exactly. His legs were sore from the morning's march, of course, but it was hardly fair to class that as pain, either.

His back—well, that hurt, for certain, but it hadn't stopped hurting since he'd donned a pack in the drill field more than a year ago at his first muster. But that, too, was a comfortable old ache by this time, and was scarcely worth remarking upon.

Nathaniel's process of cataloging his pain was interrupted as he was carried in through the wide front doors of a church. He twisted around to look up into the face of the man at the head of his litter. "Are my wounds truly so dire that all that is left is to make my peace with my Maker?"

The man glanced down at his burden, a sneer on his face. "Nay, 'tis only that there are so many who are sick and hurt that there is no better place to accommodate you all. Every church in the district around has been pressed into service."

He gave a short, harsh bark of laughter and added, "Of course, for those of you who will need the services of a priest, it also has the advantage of putting you all the nearer to his place of work."

He motioned with his chin and called out to the man carrying the foot of Nathaniel's litter, "Just over there, with the other arm injuries. May as well make it easy for the surgeon."

A fresh chill ran down Nathaniel's spine at these words. A meeting with a surgeon usually meant one thing: a meeting with the surgeon's saw—and a lifetime of dependency on the generosity of family and friends.

As the British soldiers set his litter down, he was about to ask the man whether his arm was really so bad as to require the attentions of a surgeon, but he was interrupted by the shocking pain as they lifted him from the litter onto a bench.

"Need the litter for the next man," the soldier said by way of answer to Nathaniel's gasp. "Be still and don't roll around any, lest you fall to the floor and really hurt yourself."

With that, the enemy soldiers were gone, and Nathaniel was left alone to contemplate what might happen next.

Turning his head from one side to the other, he saw quickly that he was hardly alone. On narrow benches—pews, actually, pressed into medical service—to either side, there were men whose wounds were more gruesome and obvious than his own.

One man's case would present little work for the surgeon, as his arm was mostly off at the shoulder already, a saber blow having parted flesh and bone, leaving only the sliced and stained arm of the soldier's coat holding the inert and severed limb. He was mercifully unconscious, and Nathaniel could see his chest rise but fitfully.

To the other side was a victim of a bayonet strike, among other insults to his being. Nathaniel could see no injury to the arm visible from where he lay, but a distinctive wide tear in the thigh of his pants, soaked through with a heavy fall of blood, told the story of the soldier's terrible day. This man's breath came in shuddering gasps, punctuated by little moans of pain.

With a start, Nathaniel realized that the moans of pain were his own. Though observing the hurts of others had distracted him from a full appreciation of how much his arm ailed him, hearing the ragged sounds torn from his throat as he breathed brought him back to an odd realization that he was hurting more than he ever had before. In the course of transferring him from the litter to the bench, the British soldiers had opened up his wound again, and he could hear the steady drip of blood onto the church floor beneath him.

Mercifully, it did seem to be only his arm that was seriously hurt. At some point, he seemed to have been kicked in the gut and he could feel the stiffening bruises there, but it was only in his arm that he could feel the grating of shattered bones moving loosely within ripped flesh.

He could bear to think about his arm no further, and he closed his eyes, paying no heed to the trickle of tears that welled up beneath his lids.

He awoke to a harsh, British voice. "Rebel boy," a tall, exhausted-looking man said over his shoulder. "Arm looks to be ruined. Tie it off, and I'll fetch my saw. Don't waste any rum on this one—just give him a strap to bite."

He stepped away, and a stout woman moved toward where Nathaniel lay. She frowned as she looked down at him.

Reaching into her apron, she retrieved a leather strap from her pocket and held it out toward his mouth.

"Put this in between your teeth," she said, her voice soft and perhaps even pitying. "It'll help with what's to come, lad."

Fresh tears springing to his eyes, and too terrified to feel any shame at the quaver in his voice, he asked, "Just like that, then? I'm to lose my arm?"

She did not answer him directly, but pushed the leather strap toward his lips, her expression turning determined. "You'll want this before I tie it off, lest you cry out and distress those about you."

He opened his mouth and let her slip it past his teeth.

"Mind that you don't get your tongue in the way, now, and hold onto the bench with your good hand."

He nodded and gripped the bench as tightly as he could.

She reached again under her apron and brought forth a cord, which she slid under his ruined arm.

If Nathaniel thought he'd been in pain before, now he was brought to the gates of the inferno itself, as she wrapped the cord around the limb and tied a short length of wood into it the loose ends, and then she gave him an apologetic look as she took the stick into her hand.

He felt her turn the wood once, then twice, and then he felt no more as the merciful darkness finally rushed up around him and swallowed him whole.

Chapter 2

"You'll give your parole, then, rebel, and swear not to take up arms against your sovereign again?"

Nathaniel choked on the harsh laugh that threatened to bubble up out of his chest. Motioning to the pinned-back sleeve with his hand, he answered, "I should not expect that will be a problem, sir."

The British officer glanced up from his paper for the first time, and a grim little smile flitted across his face. "No, I suppose not. Your name, lad?"

Nathaniel gave the man his name and watched as his quill scratched and jumped along the page, recording his identity upon it.

"Can you make your mark here, then, so that we may release you and send you on your way?"

"Well, I had previously used the hand that's gone to do so, but I can do my best, I suppose."

"That is all that will be necessary. I will witness it for you. Shall I read it out to you?"

Nathaniel nodded, grateful for the officer's forbearance.

The officer pursed his lips slightly and lifted the page so that he could see it more clearly. "This will certify that the bearer, private soldier Nathaniel Wooster, is a paroled prisoner of His Majesty's forces then operating under the command of Lieutenant Colonel

Banastre Tarleton, and pursuant to the usual and customary practices of war, is permitted to return to his home, where he will remain undisturbed for so long as he shall refrain from conducting or assisting in rebellion against His Majesty's duly appointed representatives in these American colonies."

Nathaniel nodded again and said, "I am happy enough to agree to that." He took the quill in his left hand, his fingers awkwardly clamped around it. The officer indicated the spot where he ought to make his mark, and he scratched a sloppy "X" onto the page.

The officer smiled tightly at him and took the quill back, annotating Nathaniel's mark and then pushing the paper across his makeshift desk to the former soldier. "Have you any effects that you need to collect?"

"Nay," said Nathaniel. "What little I had was scattered or plundered when our positions were overrun. I've naught but the clothing on my back."

The officer's lips compressed for a moment, and then he gave a sharp shake of his head. "Well, then you're free to go and make your way as you can. Have you far to travel to home?"

A pang struck Nathaniel almost as a physical blow. "Aye, that I have. I figure I've marched a good month or more since I left home, though 'tis hard to judge, what with you lot chasing us all about the countryside."

"Where are you bound for?"

"York, Virginia. It's a little port town on the bay of the Chesapeake, mostly serving the tobacco market."

"I've not heard of those places, but if you're bound for Virginia, you've all of North-Carolina to cross first. I expect you can ask your way as you go. Have you any companions among those who were wounded, with whom you might travel?"

"I know not, to be honest. I've not found many from my company who survived the day, and of those, none were any particular friends of mine."

"Well, 'tis what comes of taking up arms against the rightful authority of your sovereign, lad. All right, then, I've spent too much time jawing with you already. Mind that you stay out of trouble, and neither threaten nor molest anyone along your way."

He reached into a pouch beside him and pulled out a handful of currency, holding it out to Nathaniel as though its very touch was distasteful. "Your former commanders have made available some funds for maintenance of you and your fellows. As I can see that you are without means yourself, I have leave to provide a little bit for your travel."

Startled, Nathaniel accepted the money. He could see that it consisted of South-Carolina notes, which would be more difficult to spend than specie would be, but he could hardly complain on that account under the circumstances.

Waving Nathaniel away, the British officer motioned for the next wounded soldier behind him to take his place. Nathaniel stood and collected his letter of parole, folding it carefully and tucking it into the pocket of his breeches, along with the money.

As he walked out into the summer heat, he contemplated his tattered clothing. The breeches had been made of the best linen cloth his Ma could get her hands on, sewn as fine as her aging eyes would permit. Now, they bore the stains of both mealtime accidents and the blood and soil that had been ground into them over many hard weeks of marching and the recent action.

The fabric was worn thin in places, and one knee had an unmended tear in it where Nathaniel had stumbled and fallen. His friend Edward had promised to patch it up, but Edward had not been among the wounded survivors in the British captive camp.

His regimental coat was, naturally, forfeited when he was taken prisoner, but he did not miss it in the summer heat. Should it start raining, of course, he would suffer without it, but he could only trust to hope that he could find some way to stay out of the wet, should that happen. His shirt was stout and well-made, but it, too, carried a record of Nathaniel's accidents and injuries in the days since his Ma had presented it to him.

His low boots were scuffed and cracked on the top, and lifting his feet to examine the bottoms, he could see that the soles were very nearly worn through on both feet. He shook his head. There was nothing for it but to hope for well-worn roads and dry weather. He could always look for inns, should the weather turn, but he knew that to keep food in his belly, he would need to conserve the funds he had as much as possible.

Orienting himself, Nathaniel headed to the northern edge of the British encampment, and, taking a deep breath, he stepped onto the road that led away in that direction.

Chapter 3

A distant grumble of thunder left Nathaniel wishing that he'd been able to give a more convincing account of himself at the last tavern where he'd tried to secure a bed for the night. The proprietor had looked him over suspiciously, asking curtly, "Tory or rebel?"

"Neither," Nathaniel answered, digging into his pocket for the well-creased letter of parole. The tavern keeper waved him away, shaking his head with a look of grim disapproval on his face.

"You was one or t'other, before that." He motioned to Nathaniel's empty shirtsleeve, pinned up as neatly as he could manage.

"Aye, that I was," Nathaniel replied. "But it's of no consequence anymore, as I won't be making any trouble for anyone now."

The tavern keeper's eyes narrowed, and he pointed at the door. "We'll have no rebels here, whether you're presently fighting the King's men, or merely filled with regret for your past opposition to your sovereign. Your money, whatever it be, is no good here."

Reluctantly, Nathaniel had turned and left, realizing that there was little point in arguing with the man. The plain fact of the matter was that he had fought against Royal authority over these colonies, and his sympathies still lay that way, even if he could no longer act on them.

For all of that, he didn't want to give any unnecessary business to a Tory anyway. Better that he keep his money in his pocket to spend with a true patriot than support, by any remove, the Loyalist forces that had taken his arm.

Now, though, with a storm brewing, Nathaniel did not feel his principles as firmly attached, and he fervently wished that the question of his loyalties had been left out of the consideration of whether he might have stayed at the inn.

A gust blew from behind him, and he cast about, seeking a likely-looking tree under which he might take shelter until the storm passed. A twisted old live oak, its trunk gnarled and rough, looked as though it would offer the best option, and Nathaniel hurried up to it and seated himself in a comfortable hollow along its base.

He huddled against the freshening breeze, wrapping his good arm up around its stubby opposite to conserve as much of his warmth as he could. Another rumble of thunder sounded, closer and more distinct, and he could hear the hiss of the first gust of rain striking the canopy of leaves overhead. Soon enough, it was dripping down to the ground and puddling around his feet.

Not only did he regret the loss of his regimental jacket now, but his hat, too. A fine cocked hat, felted of good blacked wool, it was of great use in shedding the rain and keeping it from running down the back of one's neck. He was reminded of its loss on the battlefield as the first rivulet of chill rain traced a path past his collar and down his back, and he shivered in spite of the remaining warmth of the day.

A flash of lightning now lit up the forest, and the peal of thunder that shortly followed seemed to open the skies up fully, rain gushing down in great sheets now, scarcely slowed at all by the maze of branches and leaves overhead.

For perhaps the first time since the fever that had risen following his appointment with the surgeon, Nathaniel felt tears rise in his eyes. Then, he had wept for the fear that the fever would carry him off, and he would spend his last hours in agony and sorrow for the impact of his loss on his Ma. Now, he wept for himself, for the loneliness that threatened to overwhelm him, for the discomfort of being exposed to the elements, and for the ill favor that dogged him for his participation in the rebellion against the Crown's overreaches and abuses.

He wondered whether he could have resisted taking the first step on the path that had led to him being huddled, crippled, hungry, and cold. When the militia recruiter had come to town, it had seemed like a natural decision to help fill the quota for the county. His Ma had cried, of course, but she had been somewhat reassured when he'd explained that the recruiter had told him that the war was expected to be finished after one more season of campaigning, two at the most.

Confidence in General Washington cheered her, as well, when he reminded her of his habit of retreating to fight another day when defeat seemed inevitable, rather than standing and losing his men. That trait might not have endeared him to the Congress, which was said to be full of intrigues against Washington, but his care for his men gave their families comfort, and earned their loyalty.

Ultimately, though, it was his Pa whose comments had convinced Nathaniel that he had an obligation to serve. Although he didn't see much of his Pa, the family's fortunes had been greatly impacted by the trade interruptions caused by the conflict with the Crown. One afternoon the winter before the recruiter came to town, Nathaniel had been helping in the warehouse, packing and sealing up casks of tobacco.

"I recall when I had to bring in a whole crew of negroes to do the work that you and I can keep up with in a lazy afternoon now," his Pa had remarked out of the blue. He spat, and continued, "Had to sell all those boys off, though, after the blockades shut down the Charles-Town and Boston harbors. Can't ship to London, of course, and there's no sense in putting good tobacco on ships bound for anywhere else, only to see the British and their contemptible pirates seize their cargoes for prizes."

"What is to be done with these casks, then?" It was rare to find his Pa in a loquacious mood, and Nathaniel couldn't resist giving his curiosity its head.

"These? Oh, they'll be brought by wagon up to Philadelphia, or maybe even New-York, depending upon where the British lines are. By the time they get there, they'll be damp and ruined, and the man who buys them from me will be lucky to make back what he's paying for them. There is such a hunger for the tobacco that it may not even matter whether they're ruined, or even, indeed, whether the buyers are Americans or British."

He spat again. "Of course, if Washington's armies can't get enough men under arms to restrain the British, it may make little difference in the end. It's said that they can hardly find the recruits he needs to pursue the British forces, and that his generals are best at leading the British on a merry chase through the countryside."

He sighed. "Chasing about like dogs on the hunt is all good fun, but it does not accomplish the task of putting the British back on their ships to go home and leave us in peace. For that, every subscription that is raised, every militia quota asked of us, will have to be filled with good, faithful men, and the supplies to keep them at full strength must also be found."

He shrugged, and lamented, "I'd sign up myself, but your Ma has enough hardship on her hands as it is, without I should add further to it. She's not had it easy since I removed to my own home, and were I to fail to provide for her and for you, she would have no place to turn."

Nathaniel said nothing. It had always been a great confusion to him why his Ma and Pa lived in separate houses, his Ma at the top of the bluff overlooking the harbor, and his Pa nearby to his warehouse at the bottom of the bluff, but every time he'd tried to ask either of them why this peculiar arrangement had happened, they rebuffed him.

Ma always got a pinched look in her eyes when Nathaniel asked such awkward questions, and Pa would set his jaw and purse his lips, with a faraway look in his eyes. Neither was forthcoming, in any event, and both of them made clear by their attitudes that it was their private business, and none of his.

Still and all, they were his parents, and he loved them each for their own qualities. He spent most of his days helping his Ma, but the occasions when his Pa summoned him to the warehouse, Nathaniel answered eagerly.

So when the recruiter had come to town, promising a bounty of five dollars to any man who joined the militia, Nathaniel thought about what the money would mean to his Ma, and what the gesture would mean to his Pa, and signed up on the spot.

The tales of glory and honor earned in marvelous battles

against the weak and cowardly British forces had turned out to all be inventions of the recruiter's glib tongue, but until his crippling, Nathaniel had in any event found the camaraderie and opportunity to see the countryside that the fast-talking man had promised.

His hopes of supporting his Ma beyond what Pa could offer her had been dashed by the unreliable nature of his pay. He had, at least, been able to face the British forces and shoulder a musket in the service of the project of ridding these shores of Crown interference and depredation.

Shifting to relieve the pressure of the rough bark of the tree against his neck, he sighed. Though he was returning home, he was of no possible use to his Pa in the warehouse, and unable to think of any occupation in which he could earn the money to support himself, never mind his Ma. Instead, he would be a burden on them both, and a disappointment in every way.

The rain intensified again, impossible though that might have seemed, and a blinding flash of lightning was followed immediately by a crash of thunder louder than any sound Nathaniel had ever heard in his life. The combination left him stunned for a moment, and as his eyes recovered their ability to see into the darkness, it sounded like the rain had shut off, as though a pitcher had been tipped back upright.

However, he was confused by the fact that he could still feel it on his face, and could see the trees around him moving in a wind that he could not hear. He reached up to touch his ear, and could not even hear his fingers questing across it.

Into this world of sudden silence, Nathaniel let loose a wail of grief and rage, as he wondered anew what more could be taken from him. It was not enough that he'd lost an arm, but now he must find his way through the world with no ability to hear it, too?

It seemed more than could be asked of any one man to bear, and Nathaniel huddled miserably even deeper against the tree, while the rain lashed at him, and lightning continued to flash about him. The thunder, though, was denied to him.

Chapter 4

Nathaniel woke to birdsong, and it took him a while to notice and appreciate how welcome that was. He slowly and stiffly stood from where he'd spent the night, noting with a grim expression just how wet his clothes still were.

He sneezed, and the wood around him quieted for a moment—but he could still hear his feet shuffling through the leaves and branches on the ground, so he knew that it wasn't his ears failing him again. After a moment, the birds surprised into silence by the explosion of his sneeze started calling again, and he smiled despite himself at the pleasure of hearing them.

Gratitude for the small gifts of the world made suffering easier to bear. He remembered the preacher saying so one Sunday, and this was the first time he had felt the truth of that sentiment fully. His clothes stuck to him as he moved, and it felt like his skin was all pruned up, like it would get when he'd been too long in the river as a boy.

The sun shone through the leaves of the trees around him, and a warm breeze tousled his hair. The breeze on his wet clothes, though, chilled him, and he decided that radical action was necessary before he could resume the road. He pushed a little further into the woods, until he found a small, sunlit clearing.

He nudged off each of his boots with the opposite toe and scrunched his nose at the smell of his long-confined feet. Removing the rest of his garments, he draped them carefully over low-hanging branches to dry in the breeze, while he stretched himself out on the leaves to soak in the sun and dry somewhat, as well.

Despite himself, he found his gaze dropping to the stump of his arm. The scar on the end was still an angry red, and it ached, now that he was paying attention. Almost, he thought, he could feel pain going all the way down to the fingertips of his absent arm, regardless of the evidence of his eyes telling him that there was no arm there to relay such sensations.

All that remained of his arm was perhaps a third of the upper end. The initial amputation had been just above his elbow, but an infection had brought the surgeon around a second time, and the dire man had taken another exaction, leaving no more than could flop around uselessly whenever Nathaniel forgot for a moment and tried to reach for something.

Pinning his sleeve up at his chest at least kept that from being too obvious, as well as serving to remind him that he needed to use his other hand for everything now.

Now, without the constraint of clothing, he tried consciously moving his stump, finding that it felt strange, but he could control its movements. Doing so only increased the ache at the scar, though, and he soon desisted, the novelty worn off.

He'd never really thought about the workings of his body before. He'd think about running, or moving a cask, or loading a gun, and his limbs would respond to the direction of his thoughts, doing his bidding and serving his needs. Though, now that a substantial part of that was gone forever, he found that he missed it more keenly than he had ever appreciated it.

The sunlight playing over his skin was warming and

comfortable, and he closed his eyes, relaxing back into the ground beneath him. Twigs and leaves dug into his back, and he knew that they'd likely itch like the very dickens later, but for now, he was happy to let the sun work its magic to renew his chilled and damp skin.

He wasn't even aware that he'd fallen asleep again until he heard a quiet exclamation quite near him. His eyes flew open, and he found himself looking into the inverted face of what he thought at once must be a young man of the Cherokee nation, his distinctive tattoos and dress setting him apart from the smaller tribes whose sparse populations his troop had encountered on their way to join the forces in South Carolina.

The Cherokee had been a hostile presence across this country, Nathaniel knew, until the most violent among them had been pushed back to the frontier some years back. Those who remained had pledged to be neutral, and the word was that they could be trusted to honor that pledge. Of course, whether that applied to this particular man was another question, even setting aside the uncertainty over whether he was Cherokee or some other tribe.

All of this flew through Nathaniel's mind before the Indian spoke.

"What do you here, what do clothing there?" The man seemed genuinely perplexed by Nathaniel's state as he gestured first to Nathaniel himself, and then to his clothes hanging on the branches nearby.

For his part, Nathaniel hurried to cover himself, exclaiming as he struggled to his feet, "Where did you come from?"

"Am come from nowhere. Just walk to home, find you where deer are when no man lies in the sun."

Nathaniel barely registered the Indian's comments, so busy was he at dressing himself. He realized that he must have been asleep for some time, as his shirt was completely dry, and even his stockings were mostly dry. The waist of his breeches was still damp, but that was the least of his concerns at this point.

The Cherokee had a fearsome reputation, and he knew that he had been—still was, for that matter—defenseless, should the other man decide that he had violated treaty grounds or committed some other offense, or should he turn out to belong to some Indian tribe that was on unfriendly terms with the Americans.

Nathaniel tried to explain himself to the man. "I was caught in the storm last night," he gestured with his good hand to the sky, bringing it down in a waving motion to approximate the rainfall. "My clothing was wet, and needed to dry." He plucked at his shirt and pantomimed squeezing it out, hampered both in the reenactment and in the original attempt by the lack of a second hand.

He pointed back in the direction of the road. "I am also trying to walk home, but I did not mean to disturb your deer-hunting grounds."

The Indian nodded gravely. "Much rain in night. Not good be out." He indicated himself with one finger. "Am help you find road, go to home."

Nathaniel found himself breathing a sigh of relief. "Thank you very kindly. I will be happy to be on my way again."

He had heard tales told around campfires late in the night by his fellow soldiers, about the savagery of which members of the various Indian tribes were capable. He knew full well that most of the tales were likely embellished for the purposes of making a better story to haunt the dark. However, he remembered the more believable warnings of his sergeant, about men who had become separated from their units in the night, only to be found in the morning with their throats cut and their bodies mutilated.

The Cherokee had not lately been held to be responsible for such attacks, since the bands which had allied themselves with the British had been pushed back into the back country, but Nathaniel cursed himself just the same for putting himself at such risk. Once again, he realized, fortune had smiled upon him, and he reflected that it was a funny thing for a cripple to be thanking his lucky stars so often.

The other man moved toward the side of the clearing closest to the road and paused. "Am Yonahequah, call Big Bear."

Nathaniel finished the awkward operation of pulling on his boots with one hand and then stood. "I'm Nathaniel Wooster, just called Nathaniel."

Yonahequah nodded, and set off for the road, Nathaniel trailing behind him.

What could have been a disaster—or even his sudden death—was turning out to be a downright civilized introduction and offer of assistance.

"Where be home?" the Indian called out over his shoulder, though he did not slow as he moved between the trees.

"Virginia," Nathaniel panted, trying to match the other man's stride.

Yonahequah stopped. "Be many days walking from here." He regarded Nathaniel with frank curiosity, seeming about to say something else, and then turned away to lead him toward the road again.

Nathaniel was keenly aware of how strange a person he must seem to be. Alone, traveling to a destination still a fortnight of hard marches away, and found asleep in a clearing in the woods, with his clothing waving in the breeze overhead. Never mind his missing arm—indeed, that might be the most reassuringly normal thing about him, under the circumstances.

The elevated roadbed appeared between trees ahead, and Yonahequah stopped again. "Am go home now. You go home now. That way." He pointed to where the road led northward, and Nathaniel nodded his gratitude.

"Thank you for guiding me, and I wish you a safe return home." He passed by the Indian, who continued to regard him curiously as he walked away.

Yonahequah called after him, "Better be find shelter for rain, not sleep under sun."

Nathaniel thought he detected a hint of laughter in the other man's voice, but he just nodded and waved as he made his way back up onto the road, where he focused on putting one foot after the other.

It was good advice, in any event. He would try not to let any mere difference of opinion with an innkeeper leave him sleeping in the open again. If nothing else, it was better to sneak into a barn or even under a wagon than to spend another night like the last one.

As it was, the events of the night—and this morning—made for a more lighthearted story to tell his Ma and Pa when he got home. It was a better tale to share with them than the one about how he came to be back home before his enlistment was up, and why he now wore his empty sleeve pinned to his chest.

Chapter 5

Handing over his fare, Nathaniel stepped eagerly onto the deck of the ferry, watching a pair of dragonflies dance low over the water. The ferryman looked suspiciously at the South-Carolina bill Nathaniel had given him, then grunted and shook his head, shoving it into a worn leather pouch slung tight under his waistcoat.

Seeing Nathaniel's expectant expression, he muttered, "Can't give you any change out of that," he said. "Won't likely be able to get anything of value for it, myself."

Nathaniel grimaced in reply.

"My Pa has told me he can remember when this ferry cost threepence, and now you tell me that five shillings is scarcely enough to pay my fare?"

"Have you threepence in copper? I'd take that over this bill." The ferryman reached into the purse and held out the bill, his chin jutting out defiantly at Nathaniel.

"Nay," Nathaniel admitted. "The bills are all I have." He shrugged. "I've not far to go now, so I'll pay what you ask, and depend upon your goodwill to see me to the other side."

The ferryman looked mollified as he shoved the money back into his pouch. "No sense in waiting," he said. "Unless you know of anyone behind you on the road who'll be needing passage."

"None that I saw," Nathaniel said.

"Good enough," the ferryman said. "Hold on now, while I get us started."

He quickly untied the rope that secured the vessel to a post by the road and pushed the ferry off the shore with a long pole, and then used the same pole to propel the flat boat into the current.

Nathaniel watched the ferryman work, envying him for a moment his two sound arms. More than 'sound' – the work of propelling the ferry across the river against the current had made the man's shoulders solid and broad, and Nathaniel could see that whoever had made his shirt for him had been obliged to cut the sleeves of it more generously than most.

The ferryman saw him watching and smiled. "Take it you're going home?" He gestured needlessly at Nathaniel's pinned-up, empty shirtsleeve.

"Aye," he said, perhaps more curtly than was warranted.

"Where'll that be?" The ferryman's interest seemed genuine, and Nathaniel answered without worrying over whether the man was friend or foe to the cause of American independence.

"York."

"Ah, so you're getting close, I take it. Up from the fighting to the South?"

"Aye, I was wounded at Waxhaws."

The ferryman nodded, his expression now grave. "That were a bad one. What I heard, the British acted monstrously, carrying on the fight even after you and your fellows laid down your weapons."

Nathaniel shook his head slightly. "Nay, I did not see anyone struck after their guns were laid down, though there was some considerable misunderstanding about the parley, it seemed to me. They did attack us after we'd sent out a man under a white flag, but I was told afterwards that they were responding to fire from our side."

He shrugged. "In any event, once it was over, I was treated decently enough. They picked me up along with their own wounded, and saw to my hurts. Then they paroled me out once they felt certain I could do them no more harm."

The ferryman nodded thoughtfully. "That sounds right civil," he agreed. "Still, we're hearing tales of 'Tarleton's Quarter,' by which they mean that surrendering men are struck down, and the wounded finished off—with gleeful brutality, too."

"It may be that those things happened at some other battle against Colonel Tarleton, but I cannot testify to it of my own knowledge," Nathaniel said. "The battle was sharp, that much is true, and their cavalry sabers took a dreadful toll on us." He shuddered at the memory of the man who'd died beside him, and fell silent, his eyes taking on a haunted quality.

The ferryman caught his expression and did not pry further, but instead continued pushing the ferry across, the other side nearing now.

As the prow of the boat ground onto the gravel bank, he stepped past Nathaniel to secure it to the nearest tree.

"Got distracted talking to you," he grunted. "I'll have to pull it back up to the road, but that's my problem."

He pointed up through the line of trees that stood over the bank of the river. "Road's up there. You're probably still four days' walk from home, but there's enough wagon traffic through here that you might be able to get a ride."

"Thank you kindly, for the ride across, and for the advice."

"Ah, 'tis nothing," the man scoffed. "Thank you for the account of what you saw in battle. Safe travels to you, my friend, and I hope that we may meet again."

Nathaniel inclined his head respectfully in lieu of doffing his absent hat, and started up the bank of the river and through the trees.

The road was visible as soon as he crested the embankment, and he settled into the familiar motion of putting the miles behind him. He wasn't sure what he was going to be good for once he got home, but at least he knew that he was good at walking, footsore and weary though he might feel.

As the ferryman had predicted, there was more company on this road than on many Nathaniel had traveled in the past fortnight. A man on horseback trotted past, the rider scarcely acknowledging Nathaniel as he went by, but the next man who passed him stopped to offer him a drink and a crust of bread.

"We must all stick together, we patriots," the man said as he reached down to hand Nathaniel the last of the bread. "I must be off, but I wish you a safe journey, my brother."

Another horseman passed coming the other way after that. This man did not stop, though he did offer a jaunty wave of his hand as he passed by.

Shortly, though, a wagon pulled by a weary-looking pair of old mares rumbled up behind Nathaniel, and the drover brought them to a slow, ponderous stop beside him. Almost as grey as the wood of his old wagon, the man asked, "Heading into town?"

"Heading through that way, yes," Nathaniel answered.

"Well, jump on up, if you'd like a ride. I'll be happy for the company, and we can share stories of our glorious battles."

He must have seen Nathaniel's raised eyebrow, for he uttered a hoarse laugh and slapped his own knee. "Oh, my yes, I have seen war, my boy. I fought under Colonel Washington against the French, back in the year fifty-five, when I was hardly any older than you are now. I was part of the Virginia Regiment, raised by the colonel to answer the French incursions into the Ohio country."

He patted the seat beside himself and reached down to Nathaniel. "Come on up, we've a ways to go before the sun sets, and I'd like very much to sleep in my own bed tonight."

Nathaniel grasped the offered hand and swung himself up to sit beside the older man.

"Pleasure to make your acquaintance," the man said as he snapped the reins to urge the horses back into motion. "I'm Jacob Fulton, late of the Virginia Regiments, and now a common drover, dodging armies of any side to bring goods from one place to another."

Nathaniel nodded respectfully and introduced himself, adding, "Late of the 3rd Virginia Regiment, and now paroled as a cripple."

"Ah, goat spit, don't you let lack of an arm make you a cripple," the older man said. "Saw men hurt a lot worse than that go on to be respected men of their communities, once they found their places. You'll do all right, my friend."

He gestured to Nathaniel's pinned-up sleeve and asked, "Were it carried off by a cannonball, or chain, or was your arm added to the butcher's bill after the action was over?"

Nathaniel blanched. "I don't think that a man whose arm was taken by a ball or chain would survive to be healed, would he?"

Jacob shrugged. "Don't know, as I never saw a man hurt that way, myself. I suppose you're right, though, as a wound of that nature would tend to bleed something ferocious, wouldn't it? So, the surgeon's saw it were, then."

"Aye." Nathaniel found himself recounting the whole sequence of events that had led to his current state, from the initial gunshot wound to the surgeon's second visit.

Jacob nodded, his expression thoughtful. "You're a lucky man, Nathaniel. Not many survive an infection that makes the surgeon ask after his saw."

"I suppose you could see it that way," he said uncertainly.

"Well, considering that the alternative is a meeting with a priest, and an appointment with Saint Peter to follow, I should say so. You've your whole life ahead of you now, and no man can ever say that you didn't give your full measure of service to your country."

"We've got to win this thing before that will be a safe claim to lodge," Nathaniel said. "Otherwise, my wound marks me as a traitor, and makes me easier to catch when it's time to decorate the gallows."

Jacob laughed and winked at him. "Oh, you ought have faith in our General Washington. I tell you, I saw him rally his men in the face of a defeat the likes of which we've hardly seen in this war."

Nathaniel's eyebrows both went up at this remark, and stayed there. "The Colonel Washington you fought under was the same as our General Washington?"

"Oh, indeed, and he gave a better account of himself than

most people know today. Our General Braddock had been shot from his horse, and lay dying on a wagon. The day was lost, and most of us figured we would either be massacred by the Indians, or at best, be captured by the Canadiens."

He grimaced. "We'd walked into an ambush, on a road in the forest as we were marching toward their fort. They came at us from every direction, and as we in the militia went into the trees to engage them, our own regulars mistook us for enemy forces and fired on us. Then the general was struck, and all was reduced to chaos."

He shook his head slowly, the memory clearly as fresh in his mind as if it had happened yesterday. "Then the colonel rode through, calling to us to make an orderly retreat rather than stand there and wait to be slaughtered. The officers took up his call and got us organized and marching, even as they were being struck down by cowardly shots fired from the safety of the woods."

He drew in a long breath. "We lost over half our officers, including the general. Hundreds of men were killed outright, and hundreds more hurt, many more awfully than you. They did not even hesitate to attack the women attending to our troop! Our dear helpers were nearly wiped out – less than one in ten of them came back with us."

He shuddered visibly, then sat up. "Still, if not for the strength of the colonel's will, I doubt I would be here today. He has an ability to inspire men to feats beyond human capacity, and so long as he leads our armies, I have faith that we will be victorious."

Chapter 6

As he awkwardly scooped water in his good hand to splash on his face from the basin provided by the tavern keeper's house servant, Nathaniel thought about how much money he had left. It only needed to last him another night, two at the most. If there happened to be a boat descending the river from the falls, it was even possible that he could be walking the final few miles from the shores of the James River to home before the end of this day. Boat fare would probably consume the rest of his funds, but it would be worth it to dine at his Ma's table that very night.

With that happy thought, he finished dressing and went out to grab the bread and cheese that the tavern keeper had set out for his overnight guests.

Jacob had apologized profusely for not being able to offer Nathaniel a place to stay for the night, as his little house was already full from boarders who'd come to town after it was declared as the capital that spring, supplanting Williamsburg. However, he'd brought Nathaniel around to several taverns and inns until they found one with a bed for the night, and Nathaniel was sorry to see the garrulous and friendly old man depart.

They'd talked all the way down to Richmond, and he'd had nothing but words of encouragement for the younger man, giving Nathaniel a spark of hope that he might be able to find some way to be of use with but a single arm, in a world built for men with two.

Jacob had asked, "How many jobs d'ye think there might be where a man uses both his hands all the time?"

Nathaniel shrugged. "My Pa uses both hands to move tobacco casks."

"But to pack them, or keep his accounts?"

"Packing, sure, I could do that, but *this*"—Nathaniel flopped his stump around in his shirt—"was my writing hand, if ever I had learned to write and cipher."

Jacob waved away his argument. "You can learn to write with your good hand, and do ciphers to boot, should the desire and need coincide. I saw many a man relearn to write in the sinister manner." He chuckled at his own witticism, and then explained to Nathaniel, "Y'see, the left hand is sometimes called the sinister, and . . . oh, let it lie. In any event, one may learn to use either hand for such pursuits, given time and patience."

Nathaniel nodded, but some residual skepticism must have been visible on his face.

"Or, if scratching at a page isn't to be your gift, you may find that helping a drover such as myself is more in your line. There's parts of the job that are more naturally done with two hands than with one, but a clever fellow can find a way."

He turned and regarded Nathaniel. "You'll land on your feet like a fallen cat, that much I am certain of. You've a spirit about you that I like, and the world around you will like it, too. And," he looked heavenward for a moment, "if the Lord be willing and Washington true, you'll shortly have a new country in which to make your way, and that is just bound to be full of opportunities for an industrious young fellow."

As he walked down out of the town to the waterfront, Nathaniel thought again about Jacob's seemingly boundless optimism about the future—his own, the country's, and Nathaniel's. It seemed to him that there was a lot resting on just a few sets of shoulders, but this seemed an age of outsized personalities, so perhaps . . . perhaps he could let himself feel a glimmer of hope.

As though a good omen, a boat stood tied up at the wharf below the falls, a figure dozing under a broad-brimmed straw hat at the plank leading onto its deck. Nathaniel approached, and the man stirred at the sound of his footfall on the wharf's boards. When he raised his head, Nathaniel was surprised to see that he was a slave – that or a freedman, though if that were the case, he'd have expected the man to be better-clothed.

"Good morning to you, sir," the man said. "Are you looking for passage down the river today?"

"I am, at that," Nathaniel answered. "Where is your master, and when will he leave?"

"Oh, he'll be around by and by," the man said. "Meanwhile, you can dicker with me in his place."

"Your master has left you here to mind the boat and manage the traffic?" Nathaniel didn't mean to sound so imperious, but he was honestly surprised to find a slave entrusted with such a level of responsibility.

"Oh, aye," the man replied, unperturbed. "Fare is two dollars, unless you've got specie to spend."

"I've no coin, no, but I've thirty-one shillings of South-Carolina money, which ought to come up to well over two dollars of Virginia any way you figure it."

The slave scratched the side of his face thoughtfully. Finally, he said, "Thirty shillings of the South-Carolina would cover it, I think."

Nathaniel gritted his teeth. He knew that by law, the South-Carolina issue should be figured at something close to twice what the man was asking, but with the disruption of the war and widespread rumors of counterfeits, there was some room for interpretation.

"Would you take twenty? I still have some ways to go, even if you can touch at a convenient stop on the river."

"Twenty-five," the slave countered, grinning.

Nathaniel realized that the other man was actually enjoying this bargaining process.

"How about twenty-two, and you throw in your hat?"

"Twenty-three and I keep my hat. My old friend made it for me, and I couldn't part with it for any price you could afford."

Nathaniel smiled ruefully. "You probably aren't wrong there. Twenty-three it is, though you leave me with hardly enough for the night's lodging. Am I to pay you, then?"

The slave nodded sagely. "The master trusts me with the fares, yes. Fellow like you could probably fetch up some more money from any church you happened to pass by, so long as it was a patriot church. They like their wounded men, and treat y'all with all manner of kindness, from what I hear."

Digging out the fare from his pocket, Nathaniel said, "I should like to provide for myself, so long as I can. I am shy an arm, but I still have my mind and my will."

"Well, that and your service will get you a fine welcome, should you need it." The slave accepted the fare from Nathaniel and then put his fingers to his mouth, whistling with impressive volume.

He called out, "Master Lewis, I got you a fare to take down the river. Come on up here now, and we'll deliver this fellow and the cargo you had me load up yesterday, and we can get a start on the trip."

From behind Nathaniel came a thrashing about in the bushes on the bank, and a bleary-eyed, unkempt-looking man emerged, blinking, into the sunlight. A soiled rag tied around his head covered one eye, and he peered querulously at Nathaniel with his good eye.

"My man gave you a decent rate?" he asked.

"Aye, twenty-three shillings of the South-Carolina issue."

The man pursed his lips and nodded thoughtfully. "Right fair, that fare is," he said, and guffawed. "Y'hear that, Trent? A fair fare. Good heavens, it ain't even noon yet, and I'm already all full of the spirit."

"Yes, sir, you are," the slave answered.

"Welp, let's get this run going, then." Lewis stepped up onto the dock and looked at the sky. "Weather's fine, so it should be an easy day. Trent will keep the boat off of any rocks, and we can let you off where you like. We're bound for Norfolk, might make it there by nightfall, but we'll set an anchor if not."

Nathaniel asked, "Might you touch at the road to Williamsburg?"

Lewis looked over to Trent, who nodded, and then the master replied, "I reckon we could do that, yep."

Nathaniel wasn't sure who to address, so he said, "Thank you both."

Lewis jumped up the plank, with surprising energy for a

man who appeared to have been napping just a few minutes before. "Let's quit flapping our jaws, then, and get going."

Trent shared a private smile with Nathaniel, and they followed the man onto his boat.

Chapter 7

Trent was as able a boatman as Lewis had promised, and their passage down the river was uneventful. Nathaniel was more surprised by how little appeared to have changed than by what changes he could see on the banks of the river.

They passed less traffic on the river than he would have expected in peacetime, but he knew that this region was still very much on a war footing. Many men were off serving in militias—for one side or the other—and what commerce there was would tend to be more furtive than open, to avoid attracting the attention of armies hungry for supplies of any kind.

While Nathaniel settled down to sit with his back to the rail near where Trent stood at the tiller, Lewis spent most of the morning dozing under a makeshift shade consisting of a threadbare section of sailcloth he'd suspended between the mast and the rail. As the boat followed the turns in the river, and the sun moved higher in the sky, he'd find his shade gone, and grumble as he moved to pursue the relative protected cool of his shelter.

At least once, Nathaniel thought he saw Trent flash a brief, private smile to himself as his navigation exposed his master to the light twice in the course of a few minutes.

The next time it happened, Lewis called out to Trent, "I say, boy, can't you keep a steady course for just a little while?"

"Why, I suppose I could," came Trent's easy answer, "But

if I did, we'd run right into the shore at a full tilt, which would do neither our cargo nor our passenger any good, to say nothing of what it would do to the keel of this here boat of your'n."

In any other slave, with any other master, Nathaniel would judge Trent's tone to be bordering on open insolence, but Lewis threw back his head and laughed out loud at the slave's reply. "Mind that you don't do that, neither. Can you steer for the center of the channel for a time, at least, so that you need not swing around quite so wide?"

"Aye, I reckon I can do that much for you, Master Lewis." The slave grinned, and Lewis grinned back.

Nathaniel shook his head but said nothing. It was none of his affair how another man managed his slaves, but he knew that his Pa would never have tolerated that sort of banter from a negro. Of course, he also had to employ an overseer, lest the slaves he'd owned or leased at one time or another should slow down their work.

By contrast, Trent could evidently be trusted with a high level of responsibility in comparison to the other slaves in Nathaniel's experience, so perhaps there was something to this approach, as well.

When the sun had reached nearly directly overhead, Trent called out to Nathaniel, "Fancy a bite to eat? Won't even charge you nothing for it." He chuckled playfully, and Nathaniel automatically smiled back.

"I'd be much obliged," he said.

"If you could fetch along some to me so that I don't need to leave the rudder to Master Lewis, we would all be the better off for it, too."

"Of course," Nathaniel said. "That's only sensible. Where will I find the food?"

"It's in that sack over by the starboard rail," Trent pointed to the rail opposite of where Lewis was stretched out under his sailcloth.

Without opening his uncovered eye, Lewis said, "I'd take it as a kindness if you could see your way clear to bring it over to me first."

"Of course," said Nathaniel, hoisting himself up on the railing.

He observed wryly to himself that the pair had thereby maneuvered him into serving them their meal, but given that he would earn his own meal by doing so, he couldn't really resent being made the servant for a few minutes.

In the sack, he found a few coarse, round cakes of some sort of bread, and a small hunk of anonymous meat, boiled grey. He couldn't guess whether it had been salt beef or fresh pork, but it would make for meager rations split three ways.

His mouth watered, though, in spite of his judgment of the food. He'd had far worse—and far less—during his service. While the regulations called for so many pounds of bread, so many pounds of peas, and so much pork or beef per man per day, the quartermasters seemed to regard those standards, defined by a faraway Congress that did little to see to their fulfillment, as mere suggestions.

Bread of various qualities, Nathaniel had seen plenty enough of, but meat had been a relatively rare luxury. He had heard of men who'd had to boil their shoes for a scrap of something approximating meat, but the militia unit he'd been a part of had never been reduced to such measures—at least, not during his service.

Most of the meat he had tasted had been scrounged up or snared by messmates—powder and ball were too precious to waste on feeding the troops—and too often, that consisted of a single scrawny squirrel or rabbit for the whole mess. A cup of stew served out of the cooking pot might contain a single, stringy scrap of meat, and a man would consider himself lucky to get more.

The prospect of splitting this bonanza had Nathaniel feeling very lucky indeed. He brought the sack over to Lewis, who took a piece of the bread and tore off about half of the meat to set atop it. Wordlessly, he motioned Nathaniel aft to bring the sack around to Trent.

The slave likewise pulled out a piece of the bread, and he took the rest of the meat and laid it atop the bread, remarking to Lewis, "I don't think that innkeeper much liked you. He was mighty tight with the food, judging by what you carried away."

As Trent handed the sack back to Nathaniel, Lewis grunted and replied, " 'Twas enough to last us for two days, plus feeding our passenger, so I can't hardly complain about that, I don't figure."

Nathaniel swallowed his disappointment and asked, "Might I take both of the two pieces of bread that remain?"

"It's all your'n," Lewis said. "Eat up and enjoy. We've a most generous host down in Norfolk, so we don't need to stretch this out any more."

Nathaniel took the bread and bit into one piece of it. It was less refined than much of what he'd had these past months, and seemed to be made of an unfamiliar mixture of grains, representing whatever the baker had on hand at the time. Still, it was filling, and not so hard as to threaten Nathaniel's teeth.

He'd once watched a less fortunate messmate bite into a piece of ship's biscuit, seized from some British naval store somewhere before it found its way to his unit. The man had cried out and spat half of a tooth into his hand.

Nathaniel felt a new respect for men of the naval sort after that. He'd heard that the biscuit represented a large proportion of their diet, and he thought that they must all have teeth of stone. Then he learned that they had an elaborate system of cookery that involved pounding and boiling the biscuit to use as thickener for stews and the like, and it made a lot more sense to him in light of that. Ship's biscuit mostly represented a stable way to store flour for long voyages, someone told him later.

Still, he was grateful for a bit of forage, or, as was the case now, something relatively fresh, even if unfamiliar. As for the meat, he could not resent the master taking his share, and Trent was the only one doing physical labor, and so he needed the nourishment more than Nathaniel did.

He chewed thoughtfully on the bread, identifying the different sorts of grain in it. Wheat, of course, and corn, but there was also some barley and maybe some rye in there, based on the flavor and coarse texture.

In short order, he was disappointed to realize that he'd finished the bread, and he settled back along the rail to watch the shore smoothly pass by. Before long, he'd joined Lewis in slumbering as the water gurgled along the side below him and the sun warmed him through.

He only woke up when Trent called out, "There's the landing for the road to Williamsburg, there. We'll bring you right in close to shore so you can go over the side and wade in, all right?

Can't easily run this boat up onto the shore here, as we've not got enough hands to push it off easily again."

Under other circumstances, Nathaniel might have been nonplussed at the impromptu delivery, but he was too eagerly scanning the shoreline where the road was just visible. He was now an easy afternoon's walk from home.

Chapter 8

Walking through the city of Williamsburg on his way down to York, Nathaniel was taken aback at how quiet and still it seemed. Since the state capital had moved, he expected that some of the bustle and crowding he'd seen at Richmond might have been drained from this town, but he was quite surprised at just how little activity there now seemed to be here.

The sun slanted low behind his back, and chickens clucked and swarmed around his feet as he walked past one of the few residences that showed obvious signs of occupation. The houses to either side of it stood empty. The front door on one stood ajar, like the slack mouth of an idiot, while the other had suffered several broken window panes from a fallen branch, which still lay precariously half-in, half-out of the upstairs bedroom.

Seeing fine houses in such an indecent state shook Nathaniel nearly as much as the fresh graves laid out in a row outside the church where he'd been physicked after the battle. All men died eventually, and if their lives were given meaning by the cause for which they'd been given, so much the better.

A house, though, was meant to be lived in, to witness the happy laughter of children and the quiet conversations between their elders. It was meant to open up to release the aromas of bread baking and take in the fresh breezes of springtime.

He was not prepared to see homes simply abandoned, left gaping and unloved, their people removed to a distant town by no fault of the construction, setting, or suitability of their design, but only in answer to the whims of Governor Jefferson and his friends in the legislature.

He realized the he had stopped and was gawking at the vacant houses. He shook himself and continued through town to reach the last stretch to York and his own home.

Part of what unsettled him about the changes wrought in Williamsburg since his departure was the realization that York, too, could be so altered in the year of his absence.

What letters he had gotten from his Pa had not mentioned it, of course, but neither had they mentioned the shocking decline of Williamsburg, though he must have been aware of it. He had said only that the seat of government had been moved, without elaborating upon what that might imply.

Nathaniel reached the edge of town as shadows gathered around him, and he was somewhat surprised to look back and see that the sun had already slipped beneath the horizon. He knew that home was a few hours' walk from here, but he did not want to attempt the trip after dark, even if the moon that had shone through last night's window had cast enough light to let him see his way. There was a war on, and he was disarmed—in more ways than one, he realized ruefully as he considered the choice of words in his thoughts.

Furthermore, better to reach home in the forenoon than late at night.

His decision made, he turned around and went back into the town to seek lodging for the night. The tavern where he and his Pa had stayed previously was dark and quiet, but as he ventured in toward the market square outside the former capital building, he saw lights and activity in another establishment, the bottle and cups on the sign outside identifying it as a tavern. He sighed. It would do as a place to sleep, and even if it took the last vestiges of his money, he would be in the embrace of family on the morrow.

He was pleasantly surprised to find a friendly face at the till. "Why, if it isn't Josiah Pellington," he cried out despite himself.

Josiah looked up sharply from the ledger he was examining to peer at Nathaniel.

His scowl dissolved into a delighted smile, and he leapt to his feet to come around the table and engulf Nathanial in an enormous hug. "Nathaniel Wooster, back from playing at soldier boy, are you?"

He released Nathaniel and held him by the shoulders at arm's length, examining him. Nathaniel saw his eyes widen for a moment as he took note of the empty, pinned sleeve on his chest, but then the other man said to him, "There's something different about you, lad, though I can't quite put a name to it."

His eyes quested over Nathaniel's face. "It's not your beard, as you never wore one before, and what's growing on your face now scarcely merits the word."

Nathaniel chuckled. Josiah was perpetually cracking wise when he and his Pa had stayed in his old tavern, and it was comforting, somehow, to see how little had changed.

Josiah nodded to himself, continuing the ruse, if only for his own benefit. "Your shoulders have filled out, what with all of that carrying and serving they doubtless had you do."

"Aye," said Nathaniel, "Though you could say that it's been

more than two months since I've been *under arms*, as it were."

Josiah grinned in appreciation for Nathaniel's witticism, and then his face grew grave. "I am glad to see, my old friend, that the surgeon left your humor intact, and did not bleed you of your sanguine nature."

"Oh, he tried, and even came back for a second helping when the first did not satiate his desire for a sacrifice of flesh and bone." Nathaniel kept his tone lighthearted, but still noticed Josiah flinch at his description of the doubled amputation.

"So, you've been released of service to come on home, then?"

"I was paroled by the British, as I was, in truth, their captive during my convalescence."

Josiah's eyebrows went up. "Where was this, then?"

"At Waxhaws, over the border in South-Carolina."

The tavern keeper's eyebrows went even higher, disappearing under the shaggy hair that lay across his forehead. "You were there? Every account I've heard or read says that the Virginia regiment was sliced to ribbons."

Nathaniel nodded. "Aye, I was there, and that's an altogether too apt description of it. They charged us with cavalry and cut apart our lines with sabers. I was one of the lucky ones, laid low by someone firing from behind the charge before their line arrived. I almost think it was a shot fired in error, for nobody should have been shooting through a line of horse."

Josiah shook his head. "That error, if it were such, likely saved your life, though it cost you an arm."

"That's a way of looking at it, I suppose," Nathaniel said. "Still, I would have been just as satisfied to have been captured unhurt, and to have taken my chances as a prisoner."

"Oh, never you say such a thing, Nathaniel. The way the British treat our men that they take prisoner has become somewhat infamous. Your odds were better under the surgeon's knife, I'll warrant."

"As bad as that?"

The other man nodded, his expression again grave. "Since our army at Charles-Town was taken, it is said that the British forced the main body of the defenders onto prison hulks in the harbor there, and that the chief way to depart from those accursed ships is by the release of grim death. Between bad air and worse food, disease is rampant aboard them, and our envoys seem powerless to effect an improvement of their condition."

"Great merciful heavens," Nathaniel said, aghast. "I suppose I am lucky indeed to have been struck down and so given the opportunity for parole."

"Well, for all of that, since you were serving in the militia, and not in the Continental Army, you'd have been paroled even had your capture taken place at Charles-Town, as there were too many American prisoners for the British to keep otherwise. I won't pretend to know whether that was the case at Waxhaws."

He peered at Nathaniel curiously now. "In fact, the stories we've heard at this remove about the sequence at Waxhaws led many to believe that none there were spared the bayonet, even after the day was lost to us."

Nathaniel nodded thoughtfully. "I've heard the same impression from others, too. I was somewhat concerned with other matters at the time, but I can tell you with perfect authority that survivors fallen on the field were given proper physicking, and that we were treated with decent honor by all who handled us. The initial surrender, before the battle had properly begun, was botched, it's true, but once the bullets flew, I believe that the enemy acted with decent propriety."

Josiah thought about this for a moment, and then said, "'Tis likely, then, that the surrender attempted earlier was the one that is being used to claim that the British are behaving monstrously and in contravention to all accepted practices of war."

"I don't doubt that they may be doing so, and it is wholly true that our lines were mauled terribly by the cavalry, but that was more because it was a mismatched force from the beginning. Better to send a boy to face a firing squad than to send a militia's infantry to face a line of horse. The boy is more likely to leave the field unhurt."

"That was the reason for the surrender, then?"

Nathaniel shrugged. "I was not privy to the discussions of the commanders on the field. My viewpoint was only that of a militiaman posted in the first rank of those to receive the enemy charge. I may have a jaundiced view of their deliberations as a result, though."

Josiah nodded. "A sensible prejudice, in my opinion. In any event, you entered here for a purpose other than nattering on with me. Should you like a room for the night, that you may set off for home when the cock crows?"

"I should like that of all things," replied Nathaniel.

Josiah led him up the stairs and showed him a spacious room—"We formerly housed many a member to the House of Delegates in here, and even a senator or two before the capital moved,"—and then led him back downstairs for supper.

"Food's nothing fancy, but I'll sit with you and acquaint you with the events of the town since you left, if you like."

Nathaniel said, with real enthusiasm, "I would be most grateful both for the meal and the company." The ferryman's bread was a distant memory now, and he was glad to follow Josiah back down to the table. His friend motioned to the slave standing silently in the door to the kitchen, and the woman brought out two plates in short order.

After sharing the plain but filling meal, the friends sat with tankards of hoarded ale, and Josiah filled him in on the gossip from home. After the conclusion of a particularly funny story about an old farmhand and a sailor from one of the few merchant ships to have visited in the past couple of years, Josiah's expression grew more serious.

"There's another bit of intelligence that I feel obligated to share with you, though you may not like to hear it."

Nathaniel set down his tankard and laid his hands flat on the table, his blood running cold. "Is it about my family?"

"Aye, 'tis. Your mother, specifically."

Nathaniel stared down his friend, finally saying, "Well, out with it, then. Better to hear unwelcome tidings from the mouth of a friend than to learn of it from a stranger."

Josiah nodded and in a reluctant tone said, "There's been rumors that she's been receiving suitors."

Nathaniel frowned, disbelief visible on his face. "She and Pa have not lived as husband and wife for many years, 'tis true, but they are still bound by their vows to one another."

Josiah shrugged. "I don't know their private affairs, just what I hear around the town. It may all be the sort of vicious gossip that old men like to whisper to one another, and that old women cackle about when they think there are no men around to hear them. Still, I wouldn't want you to hear of it from an unfriendly quarter, whether there's any truth to it or not."

Nathaniel's mouth was set in a tight line. "I'll be after trying to learn who is spreading such tales about my family, now that I am returned." He said nothing aloud, but he suspected that even if there were some glimmer of truth to the tale, his return would put an end to the matter.

He drained his tankard and stood up. "I'd like to get an early start tomorrow, so I'll be off to bed now. Thanks for the company and the news, both welcome and unwelcome."

"Of course," Josiah said, standing as well. "Mind, you may find nothing changed when you go back."

"Naught but myself," said Nathaniel, but his smile belied his grim tone.

"Sleep well, my friend, and welcome back."

Upstairs, Nathaniel nudged off each boot with the toe of the other, as was his habit now, shaking his head at the memory of childhood admonitions to use hands only, so as to preserve his footwear. He lifted the one to look through the hole in the bottom of it, and sat on the edge of the bed, considering the prospect of walking back through the front door of his Ma's house.

Would she be glad to see him, or would she harbor resentment for the disruption of her rumored activities? What would she think of his maiming? Would the return of part of a son be as welcome as the whole man might have been?

He wondered, too, how the rest of the town would regard him. Could he ever go back to being just Nathaniel Wooster, their old neighbor and friend, or was he now indelibly marked as Private Wooster of the Virginia Regiment, home on parole from the captivity of the British authorities?

He knew that the answers to his questions lay just on the other side of the rest he so desperately needed, so he finished undressing and forced himself to lay down and try to sleep.

Chapter 9

As he topped the rise that brought the town into view, he was pleased to see that York had the same aspect as when he'd departed. The same tidy houses of brick and clapboard, the tower of the courthouse, and the whitewashed fences along the roads—all was in the same good order. The lack of ships at the quay would have given a merchant-minded man such as his Pa a reason to frown, but even that could be chalked up to a storm out at sea delaying the traffic.

Before the buildings of the town was a broad meadow, ringed by lines of trees planted by hands long-forgotten to mark off the line between one man's property and his neighbor's. Nathaniel continued climbing the rise into town until he could see over the lip of the bluff, the waves of the river glinting in the summer sun.

And there, just off the main road, he could see the modest home he and his ma shared. It was all he could do to keep his step steady, and not break into a mad run. A few people moved about in the streets, and a couple of them were familiar to him, but he would not be turned or delayed from his objective any longer.

Stepping purposefully up to the door, he rapped once, then twice, and stepped back to wait. After what seemed like an eternity, he could hear his ma muttering audibly about unannounced visitors as she made her way to the door.

When the door opened, she stood there for a moment,

blinking up at him in disbelief. Then her arms were around him, and her tears soaking through his shirt.

He wrapped his good arm around her thin shoulders, just repeating over and over, "Ma. Ma. Ma."

Eventually, she released him and held him out at arm's length, looking him over with wonder and disbelief still written large on her face. "Oh, my boy," she finally choked out, her hand dropping to trace the concealed outline of his stump of an arm. "What have they done to you, Nathaniel?"

He answered, his own voice breaking a bit, "I am all right, Ma. I am all right now. I was shot in a battle, and the surgeon could not save my arm. But he saved my life, and they let me come home to you, so long as I promise never to take up war against the Crown again."

She nodded, her eyes searching his face for any falsity, any hint of the danger that he could be taken away again. "You look well, which is no mean thing for what you've been through."

She patted his stomach. "I heard people saying that our armies were starving in the field, that they had no clothing nor hardly any shelter, and that they were dropping like flies from disease. I was so afraid, so afraid that there would come a letter or a man on horseback, bearing me the ill tidings that you'd been taken from me, and that I would never again in this life behold you."

She reached out and took his shoulders again. "And yet, here you stand before me, as sound as I could hope for, aside from your injuries. It is truly a miracle, the very miracle for which I've been begging all these long months."

She released his shoulders. "Come in, come in, and let me get you fed up, and make up for the time you've lost."

She turned and went back into the house, and he followed her, wondering at the things that were unchanged within since he'd left, and at the things that were as new to him as if they had just been done yesterday.

The table where he'd eaten so many meals was just the same, with a few spindly-looking—but solid—chairs grouped around it. The great hearth in the kitchen, a small fire crackling merrily to itself, as though the thought of heating the room at the height of summer was a private amusement, and the carefully-tended tools hanging beside it—all of these things were no different than if he had just stepped out the front door to walk down to the quay and had returned.

The pane of glass that had been cracked since he was a young boy, though, had been replaced, and the plaster that had fallen and exposed the lath beneath in the front hall had been patched up, leaving only the memory of the accident that had driven his head into the wall. A new copper kettle stood beside the venerable, old, short-legged cast iron kettle that his Ma had inherited from her mother's kitchen.

But most alarming was the change in Ma herself. Her face seemed to have aged a decade since he'd left, and her hair, once black as coal, was now shot through with strands of white. Where he had always known her to stand tall, even as his own height overtopped hers, she now seemed visibly stooped and diminished.

Her eyes, though, were just as bright and attentive as always, and she caught him examining her. She pulled herself up to stand straight, nearly coming up to eye level with him. Her expression dared him to make a comment on the changes in her appearance.

Instead, he said, "You look great, Ma, and it's good to see that you've been able to take care of the house without me around to help."

She laughed. "Without having to feed you, my dear boy, I've been able to afford to get a few things done around here. It's not an exchange that I looked for, but I am glad that my maintenance is evident to your eye." She pulled out his chair at the table. "Now sit while I get the kettle on, and then you can tell me all about your adventures since you left."

He sat as she bustled about the kitchen, a constant stream of words tossed over one shoulder or the other at him. She acquainted him with all that had passed around the town in his absence, even as her knife flew over a tightly-gripped bunch of herbs, and she pulled salted meat from a cask, tossing it into the kettle half-full of water.

She fell silent for a moment as she stooped and lifted the kettle onto the cooking crane, grunting with the effort.

Nathaniel jumped up from his chair. "Ma, let me help you with that."

She waved him away, setting the handle into a well-worn notch on the crane, and then swung it over the fire to start heating. "You sit down and let me take care of the cooking. I've been doing for myself ever since you enlisted, and there's no need for you to go straining yourself in your condition."

"You were just saying that I looked hearty and hale, Ma."

"Aye, and you do, but I am also certain that you're still healing from your wound, and there's no sense in you struggling to do with one arm when I've two good ones to get the job done."

Nathaniel could feel the blood drain from his face. "So you

think I'm useless now?"

She whirled around, crying out, "No, not in the least, my dear boy! Let your Ma take care of you for just a little while, is all."

She sat down across the table from him, taking his hand into hers. "Listen to me. You are not the first man I've seen hurt in this manner. Before you were born, your pa had a slave who was caught between two stacks of full casks as one fell over, and his arm was mangled beyond saving. In his case, the surgeon simply took the whole arm off at the shoulder, to guard against infection."

She shuddered at the memory. "Your pa sold him off, of course, as he could no longer do the work required of him in the warehouse. Poor Charles took most of a year before he adjusted to the loss of his arm, but in the end, he became quite adept as a tailor's assistant, though he never did learn to sew with just the one hand."

Nathaniel shook his head in frustration. "What does that have to do with me not helping you to lift a heavy pot full of water? Even before my injury, I would have done that with just one hand—did so on many an occasion, if you'll recall."

She nodded unhappily. "Aye, you're right. I just remember how old Charles would wince and carry on every time he moved something heavy, even months after he was hurt. I could tell that any sort of heavy labor gave him pain, though nothing touched his wound. I guessed that the same would apply to you."

"Well, you're not wrong, but I'm no stranger to a little pain at this point."

"Do you think that I could stand back and watch you do something that caused you pain, when I am perfectly capable of doing it for myself?"

"No, I don't suppose that you could," he reluctantly agreed.

"But can you let me be of use where I can be? I do not want to spend the rest of my life being fawned over like an invalid."

Ma held her hands up in denial. "I'll not impose that fate on you, Nathaniel. Yet you must confess that you are not as well today as you will be in a month's time, and that another six months will heal you further. Do I have the right of it?"

Even more reluctantly than before, his shoulders dropping in a defeated posture, he said, "Aye, I am certain that you are right. I need to grant myself permission to finish my convalescence so that I can be as fit as possible for whatever work I may yet find to fill my days."

She favored him with a gentle smile. "I am certain, my son, that you will find a worthy vocation, if you will but give yourself the time to do so."

"Yes, Ma," he said. He stared down at his hand on the table and flexed his fingers. "In the meantime, I will try to let you care for me."

"That's my boy," she said, and reached across the table to tousle his hair. He ducked away from her hand, reaching up to smooth it back down, and she grinned at him.

He smiled back, and reached out to take her hand. "I am so glad to finally be home and safe. I know that the war's not done, but it feels like I've left all of the destruction and death behind, and others can finish the job that I took part in."

She looked at him with sadness in her eyes. "You saw much of death, then?"

"Oh, Ma, I did. On the same occasion as when I lost my arm, there were dead men in their hundreds all about me." He shook his head, his eyes taking on a haunted look. "Indeed, I was luckier than I can tell you in words to have lost so little, when men to every side of me lost everything."

"What was the engagement where you were hurt—would I have heard of it?"

"Oh, I reckon you have. It was at a place called Waxhaws, just inside of South-Carolina."

"Oh, yes, I've heard that name in conversation, but I did not mark it much, other than to hope that you were not present, as it sounded like it was a terrible fight."

He nodded gravely. "That it was. We were overmatched, and our commanding officer was already trying to call for terms when someone shot the British commander's horse out from under him. They came at us pretty warm after that, and it was then that I fell wounded. The man on either side of me was killed outright, as were many others on both sides of the engagement."

He was surprised to feel tears spilling down his cheeks, but he let them fall, unashamed. "I watched men take their last breaths, and heard some calling for their mothers." He looked up at her and admitted, "I might have called out for you, myself."

She squeezed his hand, and he continued.

"After the battle was decided, they came around and picked up the wounded. I suppose that they must have picked up the dead later, too, as I saw where they'd been buried after I was well enough to get up and walk about."

"Who took care of you, then?"

"Oh, they had a surgeon with them, and there was a Loyalist's wife who was acting as his assistant. She reminded me a little bit of you, and offered me every kindness, even though I was an enemy. She told me once that she had sons of her own, and that

I reminded her of one of them."

His ma nodded. "I don't doubt that I would do likewise, were I to fall into a similar circumstance."

"I think you would, yes. I watched her weep as she held the hand of a man dying beside me. He took a fever, and was raving at the end, but she just held his hand and told him that he was going to be all right, and that his mother loved him. I don't even know if he was one of ours or one of theirs, but when he finally left this life, I don't think it made any difference to the tears that she soaked him with."

He looked up into his ma's eyes. "I do think that you would do the same for any man."

"A man in that extremity is not an enemy, but only no more or less someone's son, and I am glad to know that he had someone to remind him of that in his last hours." Her own eyes were bright with tears now, too.

She pulled a handkerchief from her pocket and blew her nose, unabashed. "I am grateful that she didn't have to perform a similar service for you, but even more glad to know that when you needed a mother's touch, she was there to provide it. I am sorry that I could not be the one to give you that, but at the same time, glad enough that I did not have to witness your suffering."

She closed her eyes for a long moment, shaking her head. "Nor would I have wished to have seen the suffering of the others who were with you. It must have been a scene from the nearest regions of Hell itself."

"I think that any true battlefield is," Nathaniel said, quietly. "How can it be described otherwise? When men strive to hurt and kill one another, they can only consider their efforts successful when they produce such conditions as would torment the souls of far stronger men than I."

She nodded in grim agreement. "I am glad enough that you are quit of that forever, even at the cost that you have borne."

"I could have been just as glad at half the cost, but again, I shall not complain, as I am deeply sensible of those who escaped that hell at the price of their lives."

Just then, there came a sharp rap at the door, and Nathaniel heard a familiar voice call from outside.

"Jane, is it true that our son is returned from his enlistment, and that he is here?"

She stood and rushed to the door, and Nathaniel, too, stood from his chair. His ma opened the door and welcomed his pa into the house.

He stopped when he saw Nathaniel, and just stared at him for a long, long moment, before he rushed forward and crushed his son in an embrace.

Chapter 10

Nathaniel tossed aside the quill from his clumsy left hand and sat back in his chair, frustration and rage reddening his face. Not only had he no head for figures, no matter how many times Pa tried to impress the basics of ciphering on him, but he couldn't even seem to control his hand well enough to form legible numerals on the page, and when he could, he seemed unable to avoid dragging his sleeve through the ink, ruining both shirt and ciphering.

Whatever occupation he might take up, he was fairly certain that it wouldn't have anything to do with keeping books for the tobacco warehouse. He wondered whether his pa would send him, too, off to a tailor to try to work as an assistant. He wanted to avoid the shame of being treated like a negro, so he decided to stick with practicing for the vocation his pa had suggested.

Sitting back up, he blew out a gusty breath. For the time being, at least, there was nothing for it but to keep practicing and to hope that his figures would become more legible. After another hour of working the exercises that Pa had set for him, his hand was cramping, his back was aching, and he was no more certain that he was arriving at the correct answers than he had been that morning—but at least he knew that he'd given it his best effort, which felt better than simply walking away would have.

He brought the pages in and set them on Pa's table, unsure

where his father might be, but feeling confident that he had satisfied the requirements set on him for this day. The rest of the afternoon was his.

The breeze coming in off the river felt nice in the afternoon warmth. He set the hand-me-down cocked hat on his head at a jaunty angle and started up the road that cut through the bluff, rising into the main part of town where his ma's house stood. When he was younger, he could remember this hill feeling like it was interminable, but with all of the marching that he'd done over the past year, it now passed almost unnoticed.

Halfway up, he saw Anna Ware making her way down to the wharfs. Curious, he paused as she approached. "A good afternoon to you, Miss Ware. What brings you down to the dock side of town this fine day?"

She stopped and regarded him, and he thought with a shock of self-consciousness that she was put off by his pinned-up sleeve. Her eyes seemed to be drawn to it against her will, and while he'd exchanged pleasantries with her before his enlistment, he now realized that she had seemed to be conveniently otherwise engaged in the weeks since his return to town.

She said cautiously, "A good afternoon to you, too, Mister Wooster. I am off to the warehouses to learn whether any might have stacked away some supply of decent quality cherryderry cloth. I need to make some new shirts for my brothers, and they were desirous of something that would hide the dirt of their labors."

Nathaniel nodded. "I misdoubt whether any of the warehouses have aught secreted away, as any goods that have gotten through the British blockade must be offered to the market immediately, just to keep the merchants' enterprises afloat. My own

Pa's tobacco shipping has fallen to hazardous levels, and anything he can move out and convert into specie is gone almost before it comes to rest in the warehouse."

Anna frowned, and then shrugged. "It may also be that by inquiring, I will encourage someone among the merchants to urge his suppliers to run the blockades with more energy. For my part, I only wish that this accursed war could be brought to a conclusion quickly, whichever way it is to fall."

Nathaniel favored her with a brief, tight smile. "For my part, I hope that the cause to which I gave my arm is victorious, so as to give some value to my loss, but I do appreciate your sentiment. The war has worn on long enough for all of us but General Washington, General Clinton and their respective lieutenants."

An expression of shy interest stole over Anna's face. "I've heard little of the state of the war, other than that it continues. You have returned lately from the active lines of battle?"

He smiled wryly at her. "Relatively lately, yes, and I was in a pretty warm contest, off in South-Carolina." He considered how much to tell her and settled for saying only, "My regiment was soundly beaten, and our losses were quite shocking, but the notices I hear of the progress of the war elsewhere are not quite so discouraging."

"I have heard that we are fighting the British and their allies both to the north and to the south of Virginia, and yet there is no action at all in these parts?"

"Aye, that is true, as far as it goes. The most recent intelligence I have heard of events to the north is that the city of New-York is still hotly contested. To the south, the loss of Charles-Town is, naturally, a serious blow, and it should not surprise me if we lose all of the Carolinas to permanent British rule, along with Georgia."

Anna gasped, her hand rising to her mouth. "Are those colonies not frightfully close to Virginia?"

"They are, at that. The frontier with North-Carolina lies along the southern edge of Virginia, and I traveled home after my release from captivity by passing entirely through that state from south to north. Still, there is a greater proportion of people friendly to our cause on this side of the frontier than on that, from what I saw on the way."

She regarded him soberly for a moment, and then asked, suddenly, "Does it still hurt?" Her eyes darted down to his pinned-up sleeve, and he glanced down at it himself.

"Sometimes," he said truthfully. "Some nights, it itches like my arm is still there, but of course, there is nothing I can scratch to relieve it. Other times, particularly when there's a storm brewing, it aches, and if I should bump it by some accident, it is still enough to draw an oath to my lips." He smiled at her as he said this, and she giggled in reply.

He did not tell her of the moments when he would wake up in the night, trying to pull his blanket over himself with a hand that was no longer there, nor of the tears of frustration and rage that would spill from his eyes as he struggled to find sleep again.

Even worse were the nightmares where he'd lost not only his arm, but his legs, and lay on the field with corpses grinning at him from every side, unable to even lift his head clear of the mud that was slowly filling his mouth and drowning him.

Worst of all, though, were the dreams where he was whole and unhurt, and living his life as he would have done had he never been shot. Waking from those was an experience of reliving the entire shock of his loss afresh, as he realized that he could never again tie a knot, or cut a piece of meat with fork and knife, or properly embrace his ma.

He noticed Anna regarding him with a quizzical expression, and shook off the memory of these torments. He shrugged. "As for the rest, I have good days and I have bad days. 'Tis like any other infirmity in that it takes time to adjust your life to it."

He remembered something that the surgeon's assistant had said to him as she changed the dressings on his wound, and repeated it now as much for his own benefit as for Anna's.

"The most important thing is to give my attention to the things that I still have, and not dwell on what I've lost."

He lifted his hand to gesture around him. "I am returned home to a community relatively untouched by the convulsions of our country, and my health is otherwise sound. I've family and friends who are happy for my return, and the prospect of some form of gainful employment despite it all."

Anna reached out and grasped his arm warmly. "You may count me among those who are glad for your return, Nathaniel. I remembered you in my prayers during your absence, and I am gratified that the great Author of our world saw fit to answer them."

Nathaniel was struck dumb for a moment, and wasn't quite sure how to answer. He had thought that Anna had promised herself to the son of a prosperous tobacco farmer from the uplands, and had no cause to believe that she had ever given his welfare any particular thought. She had always been friendly enough, sure, but that was more in the line of general courtesy than any specific interest. Remembering him in her prayers, though . . .

He recovered himself enough to stammer, "I-I thank you for your prayers on my behalf, Miss Ware. You are too kind in mentioning it to me."

She ducked her head slightly and blushed prettily, looking as though she felt she had been too forward. Her hand, though, did not leave his arm, and it felt as though her fingers must scald his skin right through his shirt sleeve.

Looking up at him, she said, "I wanted to tell you, too, that I wasn't quite sure how to talk to you, as worldly as you now must be, and I am most happy to discover that you are scarcely changed by your many experiences. I am glad that we happened to encounter one another today, and I do hope that you and your mother will call on me and my family soon."

With that, she finally released his arm, and turned to continue down the hill. She looked back over her shoulder, though, and gave him a wave in farewell, leaving him with a whirl of thoughts to ponder as he continued up the hill to his ma's home.

Chapter 11

As he approached the front door of home, he was surprised to hear laughter from inside. He had hardly ever heard Ma laugh in all of the years of his childhood, and even her smile was a rare gift in the years since she and Pa had divided their households.

As strange as it was to hear her laughter, he didn't recognize the other voice from inside at all. It was a man's laugh, low and sly-sounding, and it stopped Nathaniel dead in his tracks.

Were the rumors that Josiah had shared with him true, after all? He'd seen no evidence to support them in the weeks since his return . . . until now.

He told himself that it wasn't really spying, just checking on his ma's safety as he peeked in through the window to see if he could tell who was there.

The man sitting at the kitchen table with his ma was nobody he recognized, and he was shocked to realize that the interloper looked hardly older than himself.

They were engaged in an animated—and apparently very entertaining—conversation, the subject of which he could not make out, as the walls of the house muffled their speech just enough to render it unintelligible. As suspicious as the man's presence in her kitchen was, they didn't look like they were exchanging intimacies, but rather just having a conversation.

Not wanting to be spotted skulking outside the house, Nathaniel backed away and returned to the road, unsure of where he needed to go, but certain that he did not need to be here right now. He found himself standing before the tavern, and decided that a drink was not at all a bad idea under the circumstances.

Behind the counter, old man Garrity nodded amiably at him as he entered. "Haven't seen much of you since your return, Nathaniel. Heard plenty enough about you, but I've no idea how much of it is true."

Nathaniel leaned against the counter, raising an eyebrow at the tavern keeper. "Oh? What sorts of things have you been hearing?"

"Oh, you know, the usual guff about how you took on an entire British patrol single-handedly—if you'll pardon the expression—and lived to tell the tale. Or that you were in that terrible affair at Waxhaws, and were the sole survivor. Or that you were struck by cannon fire at Charles-Town but managed to bayonet the chief of the cannon that fired on you."

Nathaniel threw his head back and laughed long and hard. When he finally mastered himself again, he wiped his eyes, shaking his head, and said, "Well, it's true that I was at Waxhaws, and that affair is what cost me my arm, but as for the rest, it's pure bunk from end to end."

Garrity's eyebrows rose, and he whispered, "You were at Waxhaws?" He gave a long, respectful whistle and continued, "The stories I've heard from that fight have been enough to make me wish I were still young enough to sign up and strike back at those British monsters." He spat a curse under his breath, and Nathaniel shook his head.

"I've heard much the same from everyone who's heard of the battle, and it's true that it was a terrible, bloody mess, but I'd guess that most any fight of that sort is similar."

"Everyone's said that it was extraordinary, both in the mangling that you boys took and in the awful violations of the normal practices of war. They're calling the destruction of men under a white flag as was done there 'Tarleton's Quarter,' after the British colonel who ordered it."

"The truth of the matter is, I did not witness everything that happened myself, but I will tell you what I did see. Colonel Tarleton demanded surrender of our Colonel Buford, who refused. His cavalry fell upon us, and some of the men threw down their arms, and most all of us ran for it. The colonel ordered a white flag to call for terms, which didn't sit real well with most of us."

"Why ever not? They had an obligation to preserve your lives if possible, once the contest was decided, did they not?"

Nathaniel shrugged. "There was a good deal more than the usual viciousness in the attack of the cavalry, and there was considerable sentiment that we ought to at least have a chance to strike a counterblow. In any event, someone broke the truce, firing at Colonel Tarleton's horse. The men who treated me said that it fell upon him, and he took no further part in the action until it was over."

Garrity snorted. "The way I heard it, he ordered his cavalry to finish you boys off and leave not a soul alive. No quarter given to wounded, just the point of a bayonet to send them on to the heareafter."

Nathaniel pointed at his pinned-up sleeve with his good arm. "Were that the case, I would not be here to tell the story, would I?"

Garrity gave a reluctant grunt. "I suppose that the proof is in your return to home. So do you think that Colonel Tarleton ordered any sort of massacre, then?"

Nathaniel shrugged again. "I don't know whether he may have shouted orders from under his horse, or whether his captains and lieutenants ordered the slaughter, but their reply was even more destructive than the original attack. There were many men whose wounds gave the surgeon little to do but dress the amputations effected by saber blows... and many who gave the surgeon nothing at all to do but call for the gravedigger to make room for one more."

Garrity set a tankard on the counter, then reached under the countertop and emerged with a bottle, from which he filled the tankard. He pushed it toward Nathaniel, who took it gratefully and swallowed a great gulp of the rum without a word.

"You've seen things that no man ever need see, lad. 'Tis no part of the natural order of things that you should try to sleep at night with such ghosts stalking you."

Nathaniel took another gulp and set the half-empty tankard down on the counter. "What's passing strange is that it is not the dead from our side that visit me in my nightmares. It's a British soldier who was in the hospital alongside me."

He took another pull at the tankard, and Garrity looked at him expectantly as he gathered himself. He'd done his level best to avoid thinking about the enemy soldier, and he wasn't sure what had driven him to dredge up the memory now. He set down the tankard and looked at the tavernkeeper steadily as he spoke.

"He'd been struck in the chest, but survived the initial gunshot wound. He was unlucky in the fever that followed, though, and he spent his final hours raving and begging for his mother, and his sweetheart, and his little sisters, and sobbing about never seeing the green, green grass of his home back in England."

Nathaniel closed his eyes and took a deep breath. "Just at the end, he seemed to recover himself, and I found that I was hoping he had turned the tide against the fever. I watched his chest rise and fall with his breath, and thought about his ma back home, and his sisters, and I even said a prayer for his deliverance from his illness."

He looked up at Garrity, his eyes searching out the older man's as though seeking absolution. "Then, he opened his eyes wide, looked right at me, and said 'You're the one that shot me, rebel. You're the one that killed me.'"

Nathaniel drained the tankard and added, "Of course, that was his final breath. He saved it all up to pass the guilt of taking his life on to me." He shrugged. "I don't know whether he was right, whether I'm the one who fired the shot that kept him from the green, green grass of England and left him instead under the blood-soaked red soil of South-Carolina. But it may as well have been me, for all that it matters."

Chapter 12

Nathaniel awoke with his head pounding. Between the shock of catching his ma entertaining a man who was not his pa, and the painful recollection of the death of the British soldier, he'd drunk far too much rum before making his way back home.

The house had been dark and quiet when he returned, and he'd crept in as silently as he could to avoid disturbing his ma... or anyone else who might happen to be present.

Ma was not extending him the same courtesy this morning, though, as it sounded as though she was banging her spoon on the copper kettle with intentional vitriol.

She was using the heavy wrought implement to stir the contents of the pot, and Nathaniel swung his feet over the side of the bed with a groan.

She looked up at him, a cross little frown on her face.

"You smell like you drank half a brewery last night, boy. And you stayed out long enough to have accomplished the same, too. Porridge for your breakfast, once you feel fit to take it." She gave the pot another brisk stir, and iron rang out against copper again.

"I'm sorry for staying out so late, Ma. I got to talking to old man Garrity, and he drew me into discussing some of what I saw of the war. The rum seemed like a good antidote to the poison of those memories."

She cocked an eyebrow at him. "And you'll be thinking better of that this morning, won't you?"

He winced as the spoon rang out against the kettle again. "Aye, though I'll not deny that it brought some measure of relief from my dreams in the night."

She lifted the spoon out of the porridge and pointed it at him as though it was a dagger. "I'll not tolerate you following your pa down the neck of a bottle, wrecking everything good in your life. It all seems like jolly fun until you find that you just cannot get to sleep without a dram, and then when you wake up, another tot seems like just the thing to set you right again."

Nathaniel had to admit to himself that a hair of the dog that had bit him did sound like it would make him feel better, but he was enough in command of his faculties to not say anything to Ma.

Taking his silence as acceptance, she plunged the spoon back into the kettle and resumed stirring it, muttering under her breath as she did so.

Nathaniel rose from his bed, pulling on his pants and stretching cautiously. Suddenly overcome by the need to get outside, he rushed past his ma and flung the door open before retching and spattering sick all over the stoop in front of the house.

"You'll be washing that off," Ma said in a cold, conversational tone from behind him, adding, "And you'll need to get fresh water from the well to do it, too."

Nathaniel groaned and slumped against the door frame. "Yes, Ma," he said weakly.

"Bucket's by the hearth," she said crisply, and he pushed

himself upright to attend to the task.

By the time he'd returned from the well and awkwardly dashed water on the stoop with his good hand from the bucket braced against his hip, she was spooning porridge into a bowl. She set it firmly onto the table, eliciting another wince from Nathaniel as he sat down.

Her voice a touch gentler now, she admonished him, "If you need to get sick again, try to make it out to the road." She set a wooden spoon beside his bowl and went out through the door without saying anything else to him.

Moving more out of habit than any real desire to eat, Nathaniel picked up his spoon and tasted the porridge. His belly rumbled at the food, but did not threaten to rebel, and before long, Nathaniel was scraping up the last spoonful and eating it, already feeling more like he might like to live out the day.

He sat back in his chair and was just starting to relax when a rap at the door startled him. He groaned and went to the door, and when he opened it, he was dismayed to see the man who'd been keeping his ma company the prior day.

The man seemed surprised to see Nathaniel, as well, and his apparent nervousness only served to make Nathaniel all the more suspicious of the stranger's presence.

"You must be Nathaniel," the man said, bowing slightly. "Is-is your mother about?"

"Nay," Nathaniel replied curtly. "Might I ask what your business is, sir?" The cold crispness of his tone was undermined somewhat by the wave of nausea that followed, but he mastered himself and remained in the doorway with his jaw clamped shut.

"Ah, she and I were discussing a business matter," the man

replied. Swallowing visibly, he added, "I do not believe that I am at liberty to discuss it with you, I'm sorry to say."

"Oh, is that so?" Nathaniel's voice was even more clipped and brusque than before. Drawing himself up to stand as straight and tall as he could, he said, "I am afraid that I must inquire as to the nature of your so-called business with my ma, for the honor of our family."

The man gave a little start, and then shocked Nathaniel into silence by bursting into laughter to the point where he could scarcely stand up, and tears streamed down his face.

Before the man had recovered enough to answer him, though, Ma appeared, and at seeing the scene at her doorway, she came hurrying up, placed her hand on the stranger's elbow and guided him into the house. As she passed Nathaniel, she shot him a look that promised a difficult and unpleasant conversation later.

"Mister Harrison, whatever has come over you?" She guided the man to a seat at the table—Nathaniel's seat—and silently handed her son the dirty bowl and spoon that he'd abandoned there.

Harrison finally regained some measure of control over his guffaws, and said, "Well, Missus Wooster, it seems that your son has developed a theory about your business with me that he feels involves your family's very honor."

Nathaniel's face burned as his ma turned to look at him, her expression one of furious shock.

"I cannot believe that you would think that of me, Nathaniel. Mister Harrison and I have been discussing matters that do not yet concern you, and so I have not felt it necessary to include you in our conversations."

She took a deep breath, and Nathaniel noticed that her eyes were bright with unshed tears. "Your presumptions about my character wound me extremely, and we will have much more to talk about after Mister Harrison and I have finished here. For now, I think that you ought to go and see whether your pa has had a chance to look over your lessons, and learn what other tasks he may have for you today."

She turned away without giving him a chance to answer her, and he sullenly pulled on his shoes and left without a word.

As he walked down the road that cut through the bluff, he tried to get his still-fogged mind to work well enough to determine where he might have gone wrong.

Josiah had told him that there were rumors that his Ma was entertaining suitors, and seeing a strange man at the kitchen table with her seemed to be pretty clear proof that the rumors were true. That the man had been so obstinate as to refuse to answer a reasonable question about the nature of his business with her seemed to be a further demonstration of its suspicious nature.

It might have been a bit of a presumption for Nathaniel to have mentioned family honor in connection with the man's visit, but the question remained in the air, unanswered. If he wouldn't explain himself, it seemed reasonable to Nathaniel to expect that his Ma would. While it would have been more fitting for that demand of an explanation to come from his pa, bringing him into this situation could only make it even more volatile.

Still, Nathaniel could dimly begin to see why his mother might have been so offended at him for raising the question. He could not imagine, though, what other options might have been open to him. The perceived insult to his pa's claim on his ma's affections—strained though it might be—was impossible to ignore.

He recalled then the comments that his ma had made about his pa's drinking, which Nathaniel had never really taken note of before. Was it possible that the drink had been what had come between them, and stolen their domestic felicity? Nathaniel's knowledge of such matters, either in the abstract or in the specific, was next to nothing.

His pa had established himself in his little home at the bottom of the bluff before Nathaniel's memory, and so he could not discount the possibility that his parents had quarreled over the matter. Their separate living arrangements had always been a curious feature of Nathaniel's life, but his questions about it had always been dismissed out of hand—and, he realized, this morning proved that perhaps that was for the best.

He arrived at his pa's shop and pushed the door open. The older man looked up from a newspaper he was reading over and said, cheerily, "Good morning, Nathaniel."

As Nathaniel drew closer, Pa got a whiff of the alehouse aroma he was encircled by, and looked more closely at him.

He asked, quietly, "Had a rough night, did you, son?" There was no particular judgment in his voice, just curiosity and a certain amount of concern.

"Aye." Nathaniel did not elaborate, and his father let the matter drop, instead picking up the exercises Nathaniel had completed the prior day and speaking in a brisk, businesslike manner.

"Your work is getting better," he said. "You made a few errors, which I've indicated. Most of them seemed to have come of mistaking a six for a nine. They are but the inverted image of one another, so that is not a surprising mistake to make. I've set some new exercises for you on these pages."

"Thank you, Pa." Nathaniel's voice sounded dull and muted even to his own ears.

"Another thing," his pa said, his cheerful mood returning. "You may have met Mister Harrison, with whom I have arranged to expand your Ma's house in order to provide you with a room of your own? If not, I'm happy to tell you that he is a first-rate builder, and you'll have a sturdy and comfortable private bedroom well before the turn of the year."

Nathaniel could barely believe his ears. His Ma had taken up with a tradesman, hired by his pa? He realized in another instant that this theory did not make sense at all, and that he had made a terrible, rash error in judgement.

"Oh. Oh, my." He groaned and sat down heavily on the chair before his father's counter. "Oh, am I ever going to owe Ma an apology—if she lets me back into the house at all."

Chapter 13

Nathaniel quietly let himself into the house, and found his ma sitting at the kitchen table, watching him enter. Her eyes were red-rimmed, but she sat stiffly, refusing to acknowledge her still-damp cheeks.

"Sit down, Nathaniel. We have matters to discuss, misconceptions to clear up."

Nathaniel sat without saying a word, his posture communicating his shame and sorrow as clearly as any words he might have uttered.

"I'll commence by acknowledging that the circumstances under which your father and I live have caused you hurt and confusion, and that we have never been able to explain those circumstances to you. I'll also grant you that those circumstances might have naturally left you with certain presumptions about my conduct, and how it might reflect upon you and your pa."

Nathaniel had not expected her to take this approach to the matter, and he sat in rapt attention as she continued.

"When you were very small, your father and I had a falling-out over his reliance on drink and how it causes him to behave. I will not go into the details, save to suggest that you ask him about them directly, if you think they ought to be your affair. The important part is that as a result, we decided that it would be better for all concerned for him to move to the lodgings adjacent to his warehouse. He agreed to maintain you and I in this house."

Other than the detail that their break had come as a result of strong drink, which he'd added to his understanding after her comment that morning, none of this was particularly surprising to him. Her next comment, though, was.

"As we are married, we are each obliged to eschew relations with anyone else—but the chins of scolds and gossips will wag, and I've no doubt that there are no lack of scandalous stories passed around about us both."

Nathaniel grimaced but did not comment.

She continued. "My only regret in this matter is that you have come to think less of me as a result of it. I presume that some rumor about my conduct must have reached your ear, and it is only natural that with that supposed intelligence, discovering Mister Harrison here should have caused you to come to certain unsavory conclusions about his presence."

"No, Ma, there was no excuse—"

She cut him off with an upraised hand. "I'm not blaming you, though you were incorrect, of course. Your pa has hired Mister Harrison to add a room to the house, so that you and I may each have our privacy. Until you have finished your recovery and found some gainful work, we assumed that you would not want to try to establish yourself in a separate domicile."

Nathaniel nodded. "Pa told me as much, which was when I realized what a terrible mistake I had made, and what an unforgiveable insult I had offered to you. Although I wish I had not done so, I can no more take those words back than I can restore my arm. All I can do is ask you to forgive me."

"And all I can do, my dear boy, is ask the same of you.

Had I found some way to reconcile myself to your pa's nature, I misdoubt that you would ever have volunteered for the militia, and you would yet be whole and unharmed today. I hold myself entirely at fault for your losses, and have ever since you returned to me."

Staring at each other across the table, they both were weeping openly now, neither of them making any concession to their tears, even to wipe them away from their eyes. In this, they were equally stubborn.

Finally, Nathaniel said quietly, "I joined up to satisfy Pa's expectations of me, Ma, not for anything you ever did or said."

She gestured futilely with her hands before letting them fall back to the table. "Had I but stayed in a position to moderate those expectations, you might well have not felt so keenly the call to meet them. We will never know what might have been, though, only what is. So I will speak plainly to you, if I may."

Nathaniel nodded assent, and she continued.

"I cannot say whether you will hear further rumors about your pa or me, but if you do, I would appreciate your silence. I shall continue to conduct myself so as not to bring any hint of shame upon you or your pa."

Nathaniel sat and collected his thoughts, feeling as though a mortar had just struck in the midst of what he'd thought he understood about his life. He had always known that his parents' living arrangement was unusual, but as they'd been all he'd ever known, he only really took note when someone outside of the family commented on the matter.

He had never really thought about what loneliness each of them must suffer, and he supposed that it should come as no surprise that some around town would assume that they had found ways to assuage it. He thought back to the years of his childhood in this house, and could think of no time when he'd had any suspicion that his ma was having relations.

The rumors Josiah had shared with him must have just been the idle speculation of gossips looking at a family situation that they couldn't otherwise make sense of. Even if there had been some kernel of truth in them, though, was it truly any of his affair? Was his standing in the community somehow affected by it?

He chided himself at that thought. What standing did half a man with no skills and no prospects have to begin with? It was absurd to think that even if his ma had come to some means of relieving her loneliness, it would change how his neighbors looked at him, or what they whispered about him behind his back.

What harm was there, then, in turning a deaf ear to those who presumed to see secrets where there were none?

Nathaniel finally nodded. "You have never done anything for which I ought to feel shame, Ma. However, I may owe Mister Harrison an apology for the offense I offered in my accusation of him. That, I am ashamed of."

His ma laughed, the sudden, merry sound at odds with the somber mood since Nathaniel had come home. "Nay, I think he was more entertained at the absurd thought that Old Lady Wooster would have any use for a strapping young thing like him."

It seemed that with their serious discussion dispensed with, his ma was willing to let things return to their previous state. As though none of it had even happened, she said, brightly, "While you were away at your pa's, that sweet Miss Ware came calling. She brought a pretty plate of biscuits, and though she was disappointed at your absence, she left them for you."

Nathaniel felt simultaneous shocks of surprise and joy at this new revelation. "Miss Ware, you say? Anna, you mean?"

"Aye, is there more than one Ware girl?"

"Oh, not that I know. I passed a pleasant moment speaking with her yesterday on the hill, but I did not mark it in particular. I am somewhat surprised to learn that she came to call as a consequence of our meeting, particularly since she was attached to Mister Bell's son when I enlisted."

"Oh, yes, she mentioned that you had met, and inquired after your health. As for her prior attachment, she's said nothing of it, though I've heard that his family turned out to be infamous Tories, and removed to North-Carolina. Miss Ware seemed quite moved by your loss, and hopeful of the restoration of your confidence."

"I hardly feel that my confidence is the problem, Ma. It's that I've only got the one arm. No amount of confidence will let me properly lift a cask, or pull a rope, or do most of the things expected of a whole man ever again in this life."

His ma fixed him with a fierce glare. "A man's measure is not taken solely by what he can lift, or pull, or carry. 'Tis far more important what he can conceive of, what are the works of his mind. Your loss only makes that distinction all the finer, I think, and as you discover what your future may hold, it is all the more important for you to grasp that fact."

She gestured to the far end of the table from where they'd been sitting, facing one another. "Take a biscuit, and be grateful that someone has taken an interest in giving you such things. You need only one hand to accept a gift from a friend, and only one hand to acknowledge it in the spirit it was offered."

As Nathaniel stood to go and fetch a biscuit from the plate—he noted that they were, indeed, quite prettily-made—his ma added, "For all of that, you need only one hand to hold a girl's hand, and it seems that Miss Ware is offering hers in friendship. I see no reason that you should not accept it in good grace."

Nathaniel froze for a moment, and then took a bite of the biscuit, without answering her. He sat back down, chewing thoughtfully and examining the remainder in his hand, almost as though he were avoiding answering her. Finally, he swallowed and said only, "Delicious."

Chapter 14

Nathaniel woke in a cold sweat. The prior day had brought word that the British had occupied Portsmouth, at the mouth of the James River. A day of sailing and a second day of marching was all that separated them from him, and though he knew that his letter of parole ought to give him protection from British forces, he could not help but imagine that they might take him up as a traitor to the Crown, if only to make an example of him.

His dreams had been of one lurid fate after another, sometimes involving his mother, sometimes Anna, and sometimes, the whole town. None of the dreams had ended with the British peacefully withdrawing and leaving the town unmolested. His service in opposition to the British forces in the Carolinas had given him cause to hope that they would behave in proper adherence to the rules and conventions of warfare, but he had heard much since his own encounter with them that threw that into question.

No matter how confused the end of the battle at Waxhaws might have been, Nathaniel had little doubt but that the British commanders were fully capable of the atrocious conduct that they were widely held to have engaged in there.

He had gotten out of the habit of defending their care for him after the battle was through, as everyone just wanted to hear about how he had managed to survive the horrible massacre there. Nobody wanted to hear any longer about the ambiguity that surrounded that cavalry charge, or about the wholly decent treatment of the wounded when it was over. Without that care, though, Nathaniel knew full well that he would not have made it home.

Shaking off the pounding heart that had accompanied the nightmare that had wakened him, Nathaniel stood and dressed. By rote, he went to the well and filled the bucket for the morning's tea. By the time he returned, he could hear Ma moving around in her room, so he went ahead and filled the kettle and stoked the fire in the kitchen hearth.

There was no tea, of course, and no shipping could pass through the entrance to the bay past the British garrison now. Plain hot water would have to suffice for this morning to go along with their thin porridge.

He filled the bottom of the copper pot with water and hung it on the crane beside the kettle. Swinging both over the fire, he added a couple of new pieces of wood to maintain it, and then went to sit at the table.

His ma came out, tucking her hair into her cap as she did. She squinted at the hearth and nodded to herself, sitting across from Nathaniel. Taking in his appearance, she said, "You look as though you slept no better than I, son."

He frowned and replied, "The presence of the British so close to my own door unsettles me, 'tis true." He motioned to the hemmed-up sleeve of his shirt with his chin. "They've taken so much from me already that I am loath to see them take yet more."

"Aye, I am sensible of your concern. The reports I heard yesterday of their conduct in Portsmouth thus far were encouraging.

They have but occupied the town, not razed it."

"I dislike the idea of their armies being so close at hand in any circumstance, but the best concept I have of the state of the war is that being here puts them in a position to utterly extinguish any communication to the southern theater. Without supplies and communication from the north, it is inconceivable that our forces in the south can survive the winter."

He shrugged and sighed heavily. "I fear that their coming to Portsmouth may portend the final acts of a victory for the British in this contest, and having laid down my life—and lost my arm—in opposition to that outcome, I am filled with fear as I see it looming."

Nathaniel's ma took his hand across the table, trying to comfort him. "If, as you fear, the worst comes to pass, our little town will be untouched by it. Tobacco will still pass through your pa's warehouses, shipping will resume, and our lives will go on."

She gazed out the window, and added, "If, as you hope, the American side is somehow victorious, our little town will likewise be untouched by it. Tobacco will sell, ships will sail, and our lives will go on." She turned her gaze back to him. "As there is nothing either of us can do to affect the outcome of this struggle now, we will be better served to put our energies toward the things that we can affect."

He squeezed her hand gratefully. "You have the right of it, as usual, Ma. My mind seizes upon the darkest aspects of the moment, particularly when selecting torments to visit upon me in my sleep. We will suffer disruptions until this war concludes, as we have for these many years, but that will be the worst of it, as you say."

He rose and swung the crane off the fire. "Water's boiling," he said, and busied himself with putting out two mugs to fill with hot water for the morning.

Behind him, his ma rose and stirred cracked wheat grains into the copper, waiting for him to retrieve the water kettle before swinging the copper back over the flames to cook. She quietly stirred the porridge for a long while. Finally, she gave a small sigh and said, "I'll try to see if I can get some salt pork while Mister Harrison works today."

"He appears to be making good progress, despite the weather this week." Nathaniel glanced over at where the doorway to his new room was roughed-in, planking covering the space until the door could be hung properly.

"Aye, that he is," she said, adding, "He told me yesterday that you may expect to be sleeping in there within the fortnight."

Almost as though it was an afterthought, she said, "Phineas Ware stopped by yesterday while you were down with your pa."

Ice water coursing through his veins, Nathaniel answered as steadily as he could, "What did he want of us?"

"Oh, he just said that his Anna is taking lessons near your pa's warehouse, and he wondered if you would be so kind as to escort her back up to the top of the bluff each afternoon."

Willing his heart to calm itself, Nathaniel answered, "I would be happy to accommodate his request. Miss Ware is a friend of mine already, and this is a service that I can do for her father regardless of my limitations."

A small, private smile flitted across his ma's face before she turned back to him. "Your limitations are fewer than you might suppose. Your pa tells me that you are making some progress already in your studies under his supervision."

"'Tis a slow matter, but aye, I am beginning to get some sense of the things he wishes me to understand."

"Good, good. Porridge is almost ready. Will you get the bowls for me?"

Nathaniel fetched the two bowls from the shelf. As he turned to put them on the table, they slipped from his hand to crash onto the floor, both smashing into pieces. He stared at them for a moment, stunned, and his Ma came over to look as well, her hands on her hips.

"One at a time might have been a better way to accomplish that," she said, a ghost of irritation in her voice. "Take the copper off the fire so that our breakfast doesn't scorch, and I'll clean up the mess."

Nathaniel said nothing, but in his heart, he knew that he could readily have gotten both bowls together . . . had he still two hands with which to hold them. His ma could prattle all she liked about his lack of limitations, but here they were, manifested in the shards scattered across the kitchen floor.

"While you're down the hill, will you check at the mercantile to see whether they might have any decent bowls to buy? This morning, we can take our turns eating straight from the copper." She swept while she spoke, moving the shards out the kitchen door, pushing them out into the yard.

"Yes, Ma," Nathaniel said, and he felt like a child again, being scolded for having done something careless.

She closed the door firmly, put the broom back in its place, and then lifted the copper off the crane and brought it over to the table, where she set it in front of Nathaniel. "Eat your fill, son. If

I need to make more, I can."

Nathaniel didn't say anything, but carefully took no more than half of what was in the copper. The porridge was, perhaps, a little undercooked, but he didn't complain. He'd ruined enough already for one morning.

A rap at the door caused both of their heads to turn sharply to the front of the house. Nathaniel's ma frowned and rose to answer it.

A young man scarcely older than Nathaniel stood at the door, wearing a fine regimental coat of one of the companies of the Virginia militia—which one, Nathaniel wasn't sure.

The man doffed his cocked hat and said all in a rush, as though he'd spoken the words many times already that morning, "Governor Jefferson sends his regards to all men of military age, and requests your service in the defense of our state. As you are likely aware, the British have occupied the key town of Portsmouth, not fifty miles from where we stand, and are thought to be likely to move on other strategic locations in the state at any time. Is there any man in this house who is willing and able to perform his duty to our state and to our nation at this time?"

Nathaniel stood and approached the door, meeting the young man's eyes before they darted down to see his hemmed-up sleeve. "I have done already all that could be asked in the service of our nation, friend. Most men in this town have served already, and are unlikely to respond to the governor's call to action, but I wish you well in your efforts."

The young man had paled as he stared at Nathaniel's amputation. "I-I see," he finally stammered, and put his hat back on. "Thank you for your service, sir, and I wish you the joy of the peace you have bought at so dear a price. We have but to win that peace now. I have many other houses to canvass, so I will take my leave," he said awkwardly, and half-bowed to both of them before hurrying away.

Nathaniel reached past his ma and pulled the door closed. He remarked wryly, "'Tis as clear an indication as I could ever devise of my usefulness in this world, when even a militia recruiter all but runs for the hills when he sees how torn-up I am."

Chapter 15

"I do believe that we may make a clerk of you yet, son."

Nathaniel's pa was not one to pass out praise readily, and the warmth of his tone made the comment doubly unexpected. However much it may have come as a surprise to hear it, though, Nathaniel was inclined to agree.

His handwriting had grown increasingly clear and even attractive over the past months, and his accuracy and speed in working the figures his pa set for him had improved nearly as much. He could now add up a row of figures almost as fast as he could write them down in the first place, and he took no small pride in getting a sheet of exercises back with perhaps a couple of corrections marked on it—and there had even been one or two golden days where his pages had required no correction at all.

His pa came and put his hand on Nathaniel's shoulder. "Now that you can do figures adequately, shall we investigate whether you can make sense of what the numbers signify?"

"I believe that I should like that very much, yes. Adding a row of figures with one hand makes me a two-days' wonder. Being able to explain what those numbers tell you would potentially make me a valuable employee."

"That is the very reason for my wish to teach you." He brought over a sheet of his business numbers and set them down before Nathaniel.

"These are from last year. This column is the amounts I was in receipt of, and this was those which I disbursed. You can see where I figured the totals of each, and what they were in relation to one another."

Nathaniel peered at the numbers, taking the time to verify the calculations under his breath, which his pa took note of, nodding in approval. "Your receipts were greater than your disbursements. Should you like for me to calculate the difference?"

"Aye, do so."

Nathaniel scratched some figures on a blank corner of his exercise sheet, and worked through the mathematics, his tongue creeping out of the corner of his mouth in concentration. When he was done, he said, "You were in receipt of one hundred and twenty-three pounds, seven shillings, and eight pence more than you disbursed."

His Pa turned his accounts sheet over and read off, "One hundred and twenty-three pounds, seven shillings, eight pence. Just right. Now, here is the same month from the present year. Would you like to figure the same comparison?"

He put another accounts sheet in front of Nathaniel, who repeated the process, verifying the totals shown and then subtracting the one from the other.

"Just seven pounds, six shillings and three pence more in than out this year."

His father nodded. "Close enough," he said. "I think you missed carrying a shilling somewhere, as the answer I arrived at was seven, seven and three pence."

"Let me figure it again," Nathaniel said.

He wrote down the long column of figures on the

disbursements and calculated the sum by hand, rather than in his head. When he was done with the he receipts column, he carefully performed the subtraction and shook his head. "I'm sorry, Pa. I get the same figures this time."

With a furrowed brow, Nathaniel's pa re-worked the figures himself. "Well, I'll be," he said. "It was my ciphering that had the error, and not yours. Very good. Now, the question I wanted to pose to you was this: in which year was this month better for my business?"

Without hesitation, Nathaniel answered, "Last year."

"'Tis true that I made a greater profit last year. However, the plain number does not tell the whole story. In order to make that much money last year, I had to have a proportionally larger amount of receipts than I did this year."

It was Nathaniel's turn to frown in confusion.

His pa chuckled and laid down the first page of figures again. "Look at this. Last year, my receipts totaled over three thousand pounds. I was able to find a ship whose captain was willing to run the British blockade, and was quite successful at it."

He flipped the other page over the first. "This year, I was only able to ship overland, and so my receipts were only a couple hundred pounds in total. So for each pound of profit last year, I had to exert myself more than I did for each one I earned this year, few though they were. If I could buy tobacco as cheap as I did this year, and sell it as dear, but in a quantity such as I did last year, I should be very wealthy indeed."

He sighed, and cocked his head. "Of course, you're right that this year has been cruel in the overall earnings for the business, and if it continues thus for many more years, I shall be ruined. However, as a prudent man of business, I have set aside some money in years of plenty, against just such a possibility as this year's scarcity. I have no doubt that my business shall weather this war and come out the other side of it in a stronger position."

Nathaniel gave him a quizzical look. "I've not heard of any benefit from this war before now. What makes you bold enough to make such a claim?"

His pa said, flatly, "Charles-Town has been most severely affected by the British seizure and occupation. I have seen notices of the destruction wrought there as the Redcoats have converted all and sundry to their own warlike purposes. The tobacco weighing-houses and packing-houses are impressed into service as supply depots, and even those merchants who were friendly to the Crown have been dispossessed of their real property."

He sighed again. "While I have competed with them at times for the trade, and I do not understand the reasons for their loyalty to a sovereign who has no respect whatever for their positions and holdings, I do not wish these men ill. Still, I cannot but observe that their ill-fortune may augur well for my own prospects."

Nathaniel nodded slowly as he thought about what his father was saying. "'Tis a miserable sort of way to gain advantage, though I hope you'll forgive me for wishing all possible reverses on those who have supported and encouraged the forces which brought me low. What's a little property in comparison with an arm?"

His pa smiled grimly. "I do understand your views on the matter, though I've known plenty of merchants who would be only too happy to give up their arm to preserve their property." He shrugged. "I am not one such, but I am not insensate to the value they place on the years of work that it took them to acquire their holdings."

Nathaniel shook his head, a faint scowl on his face. "Only a man who has both his arms would contemplate such a prospect with equanimity. Having suffered that loss, I would never make that bargain."

"That is a fair observation." His pa peered out the window. "It looks as though your Miss Ware is ready for you to walk her home."

Through the window, Nathaniel could see Anna outside, and when she spotted him looking at her, she gave him a quick wave and a smile, her habitual greeting when she was ready for him to escort her back home.

He smiled back, and said, "A good evening to you, Pa. I look forward to continuing my lessons tomorrow."

"Good evening to you, Nathaniel."

Outside, Anna was smiling prettily, her hair today done up in a long braid, which led up under her finely-made white cap. Smiling at him again, she asked, "How are you today, Nathaniel?"

"It has been a profitable day," he said, and chuckled to himself.

"Oh? In what way?"

"I am progressing satisfactorily in my studies, and I dare to hope that I will be able to make a living as a clerk one day. I do not know whether my pa can offer me employment, but I believe that I can make myself useful, despite my infirmity."

Anna took his hand and gave it a squeeze. "Your mind was not affected by the surgeon's saw, my dear friend. Some men might have found the loss of an arm too great a setback to recover from, but as I keep telling you, you are no ordinary man."

"You are most kind to say so," he said, and returned her squeeze. Her hand remained in his as they walked, a comfortable and familiar feeling. "And how was your day with Missus Cameron?"

"Tolerable enough," she said. "I misdoubt that I shall ever be as skilled with the needle as she, and she seems sometimes to despair of me as well." She shrugged. "Of course, when she was my age, I suppose that she had her own struggles with the blind stitch and the long stitch, and it is only with her years of experience that she can so readily say when one is called for and when another is right."

"Be grateful for the ability to hold both needle and work," Nathaniel reminded her.

She squeezed his hand again. "Be grateful for the ability to do figures and everything else that your pa is setting you to," she said. "Those things are so far beyond my ken that I am filled with wonder at your capacity to so readily master them."

He laughed, the sound surprisingly happy even to his own ears. "I would not claim that I have mastered them, and my pa would immediately disabuse you of that notion. Still, I am glad for the progress I have been able to make. It seemed at first as though I should never prove able to hold a quill properly, or to write down my figures without immediately smudging them with the side of my hand as I wrote."

"I have watched you writing, and I can only imagine how your hand must cramp with how you must hold it." She stopped and took his hand in both of hers now, rubbing it softly.

Even if he hadn't cherished the sensation of her fingers on his, the relief that flooded over his hand as she found the delicate, knotted muscles of his palm and wrist was almost enough to elicit an indelicate moan of pleasure right there on the road.

Anna giggled as she saw Nathaniel's eyes roll back and his jaw sag, and she released his hand. He groaned, and with laughter in her voice, she teased, "People will talk if they see you carrying on like that."

"Let them talk," he retorted. "That felt heavenly. I had no idea that my hand was so abused by the mere writing of figures."

She turned to continue walking up the hill and held out her hand. He took it and followed her, but he still wished that she would stop and again take up the pampering she had started. Other than holding hands and the occasional quick embrace as they greeted or farewelled, it was as much as she'd touched him since they had started walking together each day.

Though it was their handholding that caused the most tongues to wag in gossip around the town, it was their conversations as they walked that were even more meaningful to Nathaniel. Anna had a knack for seeing the whole of a problem, and finding whatever positive aspect it might possibly present.

Nathaniel had been cruelly wounded, and lost an arm? Anna pointed out that he still had his youth, and a span of years that stretched out before him like the open ocean, upon which he might chart any path he could dream of.

His parents' division from one other was bewildering and awkward? They both yet lived, and though they would likely never reconcile, neither were they engaged in the sort of open, grim marital warfare that one sometimes saw.

The war went badly, with word now of one of their most dashing and bold generals in the northern colonies having gone over to the enemy, in a plot to betray Washington himself? The plot had failed, and the man's treason was now known to all, and his name become synonymous with any vile servant of a tyrannical king.

The Redcoats held much of their southern colonies under military occupation, and were engaging in cruel retribution against those who had opposed them? At least they were not here in Virginia and exhibited no visible interest in coming here.

Today, as usual, Nathaniel unburdened himself with her as they walked. "With the change in the seasons, it seems that I can feel every storm coming," he said, rubbing the site of his amputation through his shirt. "It aches, and itches, and in the night, I can sometimes scarcely sleep for how much it makes me toss and turn."

She put a comforting hand on his shoulder and let him talk. On this topic, she never tried to tell him there was a silver lining to be found. He appreciated that she just listened and never made him feel as though he ought not think or talk about it.

His father once accused him of drowning himself in such recollections, and his mother was too often inclined to burst into tears anytime he spoke so frankly of his loss. Only with Anna could he freely discuss his thoughts and memories, and the burdens of his heart over his lost arm.

"When I can sleep, I have nightmares of the day it happened. I can see the Redcoats charging forward with their sabers drawn, and I can feel the stock of my gun at my cheek, smell the powder in my frizzen, pick my target . . . and then I am falling, and my arm is falling, and my gun is falling. The only thing that remains upright is the British soldier I killed, and he is just staring at me, and showing me where he bleeds onto the soil."

He frowned. "I remember so clearly when I fired. I did not have time to mark where my ball might have gone before I was struck, but the curious thing is that I do not remember seeing any of the enemy with the musketry presented to us. It was a saber charge only, with the infantry behind their line of horse."

His brow furrowed, and he shook his head violently, as though trying to force thoughts to collide within his skull and present themselves in a new arrangement.

And then they did.

He stopped dead in the road and turned to stare out over the river, trying to make sense of the understanding that had burst over him.

He turned back to Anna, an expression of wonder on his face. "I remembered just now that when the nurse cut the sleeve off my shirt in preparation for my interview with the surgeon, she remarked to the woman helping her that it was curious how there was a smaller tear on the back than in the front."

He looked down at the spot where his wound would have been had the arm still been present, as though he could still see it all these months later. He looked back up at Anna, whose expression reflected concern and uncertainty.

"She wasn't talking about my sleeve, Anna. She was talking about my arm. It wasn't the British who shot me. It must have been someone behind me, someone on our own line."

Chapter 16

"Just as Washington was most grievously wounded by one of his trusted companions, Ma, so it seems was I."

Sitting at the breakfast table with a bowl of porridge—today, sweetened with a touch of molasses his pa had sent him home with a fortnight ago—Nathaniel was describing the realization that had struck him as he walked with Anna the prior day.

She said nothing, sipping thoughtfully at her ersatz tea for a long moment. Though genuine tea remained unavailable, she'd collected what looked to Nathaniel like weeds, drying and cutting them to make a bitter, hot brew that she now took in the place of her tea. For his part, Nathaniel preferred honest, plain hot water.

Finally, she spoke. "It doesn't change anything in your current state, nor will you be able to seek redress from whomever it was who fired the shot that struck you, even if you could identify the man. Indeed, it is even possible that you were actually struck by a British ball, and mistook the surgeon's assistant's meaning somehow."

Nathaniel started to respond, but she held up a hand to forestall his protests.

"I wasn't there, I know, and from what you've previously said about the action where you were wounded, there was chaos enough that anything of this nature could have happened. I will ask you to consider, though, whether it truly would change anything, were you to be able to develop some definite proof of what you suspect?"

Nathaniel grimaced and said reluctantly, "Nay. You are right in that. My arm is gone, either way, and the man who did me the injury is likely gone, as well, no matter what color coat he wore." His indignation at the revelation that he'd likely been injured by one of his own companions in arms was already fading at her reasonable words.

He shrugged, feeling somehow defeated. "If I could look the man in the eye, I don't even know what satisfaction I might demand of him. Asking that he sacrifice his own arm would not restore me, only leave two of us crippled. Any apology he might offer would be cold comfort when I contemplate my stump."

Thoughtfully, he added, "I suppose something in me believed somehow that finding out how I was so maimed would make it easier to bear, but you have the right of it in saying that I remain wounded regardless."

He stood, his palm flat on the table. "I should get to Pa's to work on my ciphers. I am starting on the *Hodder's Arithmetick* that Pa secured for me, though it would be far easier to make use of it, could I read the text of it. Still, he is rendering that portion of it in spoken words for me, and then explaining it at as much length as I require to make sense of it."

"I had heard him say that he was trying to secure a copy of that for your use. I am happy to hear that he was able to do so—it sounds as though it is a frightfully complex, but utterly indispensable aid to your education in the numbers."

"Aye, that is how he has represented it to me, as well. I

suppose that he'll be expecting me to take over the books for the warehouse at some time."

She smiled at her son, saying, "I shouldn't doubt that is the case, though he likely has even higher aspirations for you than that, in the fullness of time."

He gave her a doubtful look. "Without two hands, that seems out of reach, if you'll pardon the expression. I should also need to learn my letters, and a decent hand." His expression turned thoughtful. "Though I have already learned to write numbers reasonably well, even with my writing hand moldering somewhere in South-Carolina."

His ma wrinkled up her nose at the unpleasant mental image he presented, and said simply, "Each thing in its turn. You'd best be off, though."

He nodded and slipped his cap on, the one-handed exercise now unconscious to him, thanks to the effort he put into learning how to do it. The knit cap kept his ears warmer than did the cocked hat he favored most of the time, and was less controversial among the few residents of the town who maintained loyalty to the Crown. With the British so nearby, it had seemed prudent to avoid drawing attention to himself in this small matter.

"See you tonight, Ma," he said, and went out into the road, where the early morning rays of the sun slowly warmed the surface of the road, raising steam into the air.

Walking down into the sunrise, he had to squint to see the river, and was unsurprised to see that there were no ships at the quay. There had been none for some time, but his pa kept hoping that someone would brazenly run the British blockade soon, and the warehouse full of tobacco could be converted into money—and not the increasingly worthless paper money issued by the Congress, either, but the real stuff that clinked when you put it into a purse, and rang clear when bounced on a countertop.

Of course, anything passing by the British stronghold at Portsmouth would have to escape their notice not once, but twice, and Nathaniel privately thought that the chances of selling the tobacco before the end of the war were slim at best, unless they again committed to sending it overland.

A low fog lay over the river, drifting and thinning as the sun struck it, and for a moment, Nathaniel imagined that he saw a great fleet of ships sailing up the river from the bay. The mist cleared away in a passing breeze, though, revealing that his vision had been just a specter, and that the surface of the river danced with reflected sunlight, and not a formation of ships visiting for some unknown purpose.

Chapter 17

As Nathaniel and his pa worked on practicing the more advanced arithmetic in the book, a visitor hurried in, speaking immediately, without any words of greeting or other polite niceties. "Martin, have you heard what that traitor Arnold did to Richmond?"

"Nay, I have not."

"He came at it from the river last week, sailing up under cover of darkness. When he arrived, he set the British soldiers loose on the city, burning and sacking as they went. I have been told that not a single structure still stands in our capital, and Arnold is the author of its destruction."

Nathaniel gasped at hearing this. "Why, I was just there a few months ago, on my way back home. The whole city has been put to the flame?"

The visitor nodded gravely, and Nathaniel's pa shook his head slowly. "Mister Richards, you must be cautious about sharing such rumors without any proof. If events are as you've described, we will hear directly from those who have witnessed them for themselves soon enough. Until then, you may just be starting a panic based on hearsay."

The visitor stuck his jaw out defiantly. "Martin, the man I spoke to about this just came from Richmond yesterday. Arnold has destroyed it, I tell you. What's more, he is burning and looting his way back down the river. The Westham foundry is gone, and Warwick has likewise been burned."

Nathaniel and his pa both gawped at Mister Richards, who added, "I am come not to spread rumors or cause panic, but to prepare for the defense of this town."

Pa was the first to recover himself enough to ask, "Should we send the women elsewhere, do you think?"

"Where would they go, Martin? We know not where Arnold will care to go next. It's said that Governor Jefferson has commanded Colonel Matthews to harry Arnold's forces, but he has only a couple of hundreds of men under arms, while it is said that Arnold has thousands."

Nathaniel's pa gave a long, slow whistle by way of reply. "And how are we to defend this town against a force of thousands? I think that if Arnold decides to destroy York-Town, he will do so no matter what we might say about the matter."

Mister Richards looked grim but did not answer immediately.

Nathaniel asked, "Have we any intelligence that leads us to believe he might come this way?"

"'Tis hard to know, as he is apparently putting all to fire in some places, and contenting himself with looting and terrorizing in others."

"Is there anything we could offer as a defense of the town, should he approach?" Nathaniel's pa had a serious expression on his face, and Nathaniel could see the vein at the side of his forehead pulsing, the only indicator his pa usually gave of extreme emotion.

"I know not whether we could offer an effective defense, but after what happened in Richmond, it seems that we must do whatever we can. The residents there offered no organized resistance when Arnold's forces arrived, and yet he ordered the whole place put to the torch after he had seized what he wanted from both public stores and private homes."

A chill ran down Nathaniel's spine as he considered what that must have meant for the people who had been so accommodating to him. Jacob, the drover with a house full of boarders. The keeper of the tavern where he'd lodged for the night. The industrious Trent and his one-eyed master. All dispossessed and turned out to find homes in the blink of an eye?

That it was an infamous traitor who had done this only added salt to an already painful wound. Nathaniel wondered whether Jacob, the veteran who'd served under Washington, had survived the conflagration. He thought, too, about how great his enmity must be for the man who tried to betray his hero to the British and then destroyed his town.

Deep in his own thoughts, he heard his name, and Nathaniel realized then that his pa had addressed him directly. "I'm sorry, Pa, what was that?"

"I asked whether you would be willing to serve to lead those unfit or unwilling to participate in the defense of the town in whatever direction seems to be the safest, should the enemy approach."

Two competing thoughts strove for supremacy in Nathaniel's mind before he answered. First, his pa considered him competent to lead such a fraught effort. However, his pa also considered him as being among those unfit to help defend the town. Regardless of the truth of the observation, it still stung to hear it stated so baldly.

However, the thought of being able to actively see to the

safety of his ma and Anna, among others, won out over the shame of being grouped with the infirm, and he answered, "Of course, Pa. It would be an honor to guide them to whatever safety there may be available."

His pa nodded briskly, and turned back to Mister Richards. "We must consider that Arnold and his forces will have artillery and so many men as to be able to reduce any direct defense immediately. We can but hope that we may harry them enough to make the cost of taking the town too high to bother with."

"We must be prepared, too, Martin, for the possibility that Arnold will have no interest in taking the town intact, but will only wish to destroy it, and so deny its use to anyone. There was no benefit to the British army in his destruction of Richmond, just destruction for the sake of destruction."

Nathaniel's pa answered, "General Arnold is too martial-minded to do things without some strategic benefit. Should he arrive here, we must focus our efforts on preserving the town if he means to use it for his own purposes, and rendering the cost of taking it as high as possible. If he means to destroy it, I believe that we ought fall back and let him practice his fell arts on an empty town. We can replace buildings, refill warehouses, and recover our homes . . . but only if we survive."

He turned back to Nathaniel. "In either event, our work will be easier and more certain if we don't need to be concerned about the security of our wives, daughters, and infirm. I believe that you are the best person to ensure that they are kept out of the way of whatever harm Arnold might mean to visit upon us."

"Thank you for your faith in me, Pa. I will do my best, if it comes to that."

Chapter 18

"Wake up, Nathaniel, and go outside as fast as ever you can."

His ma's words, following a sharp rap at his new bedroom door, jerked Nathaniel out of a sound sleep, and he practically leapt into his breeches, buttoning them up as he opened the door.

"What is it, Ma?"

"There are men approaching town, and you're needed to make ready our escape, should they prove to carry word of a British approach. They look to be in uniforms."

As he moved toward the door, Nathaniel said over his shoulder, "Ours or theirs?"

"Couldn't tell yet. Either way, we may need to be ready to leave. I've sent little Hiram Walker to run and tell the others so they can begin preparations, should it become necessary."

"Good, thank you. I'll go and see if I can learn the truth of this alarm."

Walking up the road to where several men stood regarding the approaching strangers, Nathaniel joined them. Mister Richards was there, his arms crossed over his chest, outwardly projecting calm resolve. The events of the next few minutes, though, could prove decisive in the fate of the town, and Nathaniel doubted very much that the militia commander was actually as calm or as confident as he was trying to appear.

The strangers reined their horses to a stop, and their leader swung down from his mount. Striding forward, he bowed respectfully to Mister Richards, guessing correctly that his comments should be addressed to him as the defender of the town.

Nathaniel noted at once that the man wore the blue coat and buff facing of a general officer of the Continental Army, and he instinctively stood a little straighter. He didn't recognize the exact rank the stranger held, as he'd never directly met anyone of higher rank than a colonel during his service. The white sash the man wore across his chest was completely unfamiliar to Nathaniel, but he guessed that it signified some particular honor or achievement.

"I am the Marquis de Lafayette, at your service, *monsieur*. I am sent by his Excellency General Washington to assess the defenses of this town. I am also to learn anything I can from you of the British movements in the surrounding area."

The man's accent was unfamiliar to Nathaniel, as well, though it was not difficult to understand him. The stranger appeared to be only a couple of years older than Nathaniel himself, despite his displayed rank. His eyes held a lively intelligence, and his bearing exhibited humility despite his high rank.

Mister Richards introduced himself as "Captain Richards," and added, "We were hoping that you could tell us what you know of the activities of the enemy forces in the area. We have heard all manner of wild tales, and we don't know whether to run outright, or prepare to fight."

"I will tell you what I can, *monsieur*, but they are everywhere on the move. We have so far contained them only by the most difficult of efforts. Most recently, I joined with General von Steuben and the militia commanders in the defense of what remains of Richmond. As you have likely heard, there is not much there, but what they could find, the British meant to take. The regulars have marched out into the countryside to conduct raids, but our men have been able to constrain their movements."

Captain Richards encouraged the young general with a raised eyebrow, and the other man went on.

"General von Steuben and his men fought a spirited battle at Blandford, a town I suppose you know?"

Captain Richards nodded, and the general continued. "They attacked a much larger British force under General Phillips. On retreating across the bridge there, they took up the planks, which slowed the British chasing his forces sufficiently to convince them to give up the pursuit."

"Is the traitor Arnold no longer in command, then?"

"No, that one is now subordinate to General Phillips, but remains here with his men. He has been active in continuing in his foul crimes against these parts, however. His Excellency the General has placed a bounty of five thousand guineas upon Arnold's head."

"Aye, we had received word of the reward, but it would take a master stroke of good fortune for any here to have a chance to collect it."

Lafayette nodded gravely. "I am under orders from General Washington to hang Arnold as a traitor if I ever can lay hands upon him. His attempt to give over his Excellency to the British was a terrible enough stroke, but his unwarranted destruction of Richmond has violated all normal practices of war, and he must answer for his crimes."

Captain Richards gave the general a look of approval. "I hope that you are successful in that pursuit, sir. Arnold cannot be brought back into our good graces, and the damage he has done to our country aggrieves us all. It is only to be hoped that the example of his death may be instructive to any who may contemplate such treachery in the future."

"Indeed. Now, I have but a short time to spend in learning what I can of how this town is placed and what natural defenses it may possess. Can you acquaint me with both?"

"Of course, sir. I would be honored to conduct you through the few roads we have, and to demonstrate the potential defenses here to you."

They moved away, the local militia commander speaking animatedly to the Marquis, who, for his part, looked serious and attentive. Nathaniel walked over to where the general's companions stood holding their horses' leads and letting them graze while they waited.

He asked one of them, "Do you believe that the British will come here?"

The man, a junior officer by his epaulets, replied, "It seems inevitable that they must at least pass through, given their movements to date. The Marquis certainly must believe so, else he would not spend his time taking the measure of the place."

"Are there any measures that we ought be taking to prepare for the possibility of their arrival?"

The officer looked Nathaniel over pointedly. "You appear to have already given nearly your full measure of service to the cause, friend. What is your part in this?"

Nathaniel drew himself up proudly. "I am responsible for

organizing and leading the evacuation of those who cannot fight, should the need arise. I may no longer be able to bear a musket, but I can readily enough discharge these duties with but one arm."

The officer smiled at him, saying, "I meant no offense by my words, and I am glad to see that this important task is laid upon a man as competent as you."

Nathaniel relaxed a tiny fraction, but pressed the officer again. "Are we in immediate peril? Should I begin putting into action the plans I've laid with the evacuees?"

After the initial flurry of preparation, the months of waiting and grasping at any hint of news, he could feel the readiness of the early part of the year slipping away, as families dug into supplies that had been set aside for evacuation, and wagons placed for rapid use on the roads were needed for the normal activities of the town.

"There is no safe place where you could go," the officer said bluntly, unknowingly reiterating the conversations that Nathaniel and Captain Richards had shared. "If the British arrive, try to hie off in the opposite direction, whatever that may be, but until then, there is little you might do."

Nathaniel nodded. "That was our thought, as well, but 'tis good to hear it confirmed by someone with more experience and training than I have."

"You've been in battle?" The officer gestured toward Nathaniel's hemmed-up sleeve.

"I have, yes, at Waxhaws."

The officer's eyebrows went up, and he said, "That was a hard action to have survived, from the accounts and dispatches I've heard. You have far more practical experience than I do. I've only heard the cannon from a safe distance, though since joining the

Marquis' detachment this past fortnight, I expect that I shall soon enough have more experience than I desire."

The man shook his head, remarking almost under his breath, "I couldn't get myself attached to someone like General Gates, who believes in watching battles from a safe distance, oh, no."

He gave Nathaniel a rueful smile. "Never mind me. Here comes the general now, so we'll likely be off. Best of good fortune to you in your duties, friend."

"And to you, too, sir."

Lafayette strode up to his horse and leapt onto its back, seemingly propelled by some manner of bowspring in his legs. "I have paid my respects to your militia captain, and have learned what I needed to learn. Let us return as quickly as we can, before that devil Phillips decides to strike somewhere new. *Au revoir!*"

Watching the men ride off down the road toward Williamsburg, Nathaniel couldn't help but think that York-Town had not seen the last of them.

Chapter 19

Nathaniel was out for a walk in the woods with Anna when the British general sailed into town. The cicadas called to one another around them, and the young couple were discussing their future together. Though neither had broached the subject of marriage openly, the matter was assumed to be settled, needing only the right moment, and permission from her parents.

"I know not whether I can hope to take over my father's business," Nathaniel said. "We've had to give up all of our warehouse hands just to keep food on the table, and Pa does most everything himself. While he's been doing his best to teach me, there are some things that I simply cannot do."

"Surely your pa could purchase a replacement warehouse boy or two, once this awful war is concluded?"

Nathaniel looked at her doubtfully. "I don't know whether there is enough money left for such a project. If we are somehow victorious, I suppose that I will have some sort of sick and hurt pension, and that will help, but likely not enough to solve this problem."

"You could always hire a boy or two, until the business is producing enough to support a more permanent investment," she suggested.

He looked over at her approvingly. "Now, that idea is not

without merit."

Just then, they heard the bell of the church begin pealing out an alarm, and they both looked up in the direction of town, fear written on their features.

"We must fly," said Nathaniel, and took her hand to begin dodging through the trees, back into town.

As they reached the road, Anna stopped, panting heavily and resting her hands on her knees. "Let me just catch my breath. The women know what to do, if it's the worst, and if not, it will wait for us well enough."

"Yes, but I ought be there. Catch your breath, sure, but then let us be off as briskly as we both can manage."

"Aye, my dear friend." She stood up and smiled at him. "My breath is caught enough to continue, and I know that you feel the obligations upon you, so let us be off."

"Thank you, my love." The word slipped out before he even recognized it on his own lips, and she froze for a moment, a half-smile on her face.

Finally, she said, "I like the sound of that, but there will be time to delve further into it another day. Today, we have responsibilities."

Nathaniel nodded, not trusting himself to say anything more just then.

As they hurried along the road into town, he wracked his brain for an explanation of what had prompted him to use that word in this moment. Finding no answers there, he looked for answers, at least, to the question of what had aroused the town, as they crested the rise that brought it into view.

No column of smoke arose from any unexpected quarter,

and there did not appear to be any hullabaloo on the roads around town. As they continued up the hill to where he could see the river, though, he saw the answer, and he and Anna crouched beside a house overlooking the lower town to observe without being seen.

A small pinnace was docked at the quay, a banner of the Royal Navy streaming out from its mast in the breeze. In the part of town below the bluff, Nathaniel could see a small party of red-coated British soldiers forming a protective phalanx around a man adorned with epaulets so large and brilliantly gold that they were easily visible from where he and Anna stood.

"That must be a British general," he whispered to Anna, then realized that he probably didn't need to worry about being heard from this distance. "But the force of men with him doesn't appear to be large enough to represent an invasion."

None of the townspeople were visible on the roads below, and for that matter, Nathaniel and Anna hadn't seen anyone about in the upper portion of town, either. The British officer was speaking to one of his companions, pointing at the bluff and then turning and peering out at the river. He gestured at the road up from the lower town, and the party began moving in that direction.

Nathaniel, seeing their intent in an instant, grabbed Anna's hand and pulled her back around to the front of the house they'd crouched beside. Knocking lightly at the door, he slipped it open and pulled Anna inside behind him, his fear of being caught outside overriding his normal politeness and respect for the property of others.

Inside, the shutters were closed, and the house was gloomy and quiet. Nathaniel didn't remember whose house they had been at, and nothing inside gave away the identity of the owner, but whoever it was, they appeared to be out.

Still saying nothing, he jerked his head toward a window to direct Anna to join him at it. He walked up to the windowsill and leaned forward, peering out through the gap between the shutters to see whether he could spot the British party from inside.

A sharp squeak from Anna brought his attention back indoors in a flash, and he whirled around to see the old widow Missus James standing with a sharp-looking kitchen knife in one hand, and a hearthplace poker in the other. She squinted at the two of them in the half-light, and said with a quiet tone of menace, "I can't see much, but if either of you moves a hair, I'll slice you to ribbons."

"Missus James, it's me," Nathaniel said to her in scarcely more than a whisper.

"That's what they all say," the woman responded, waving the point of her knife closer to the young couple.

Anna squeaked again as the knife passed under her nose, and Nathaniel pushed her behind himself, his good arm then flashing out to snag the knife out of Missus James' hand.

"Why, you young rapscallion," she cried out, and swung the poker with deadly intent.

Her strength was better than her vision, though, and she succeeded only in embedding the heavy, sharp implement into the frame of the window behind him.

Anna called out to her in a low voice as she struggled to free the poker from the wood, "Missus James, it's me, Anna, and my friend Nathaniel."

The old woman stopped and peered at the girl. "Why didn't you say so from the first, Miss Ware?" She released her grip on the poker, and it fell from the wall with a clatter. "And what are you two doing in my home, without having invited you and had time to dress proper?"

Anna answered for them, "Missus James, the British are at large in the town, so we took refuge in the first building that offered any place to conceal ourselves. We are at least as upset as you are at their intrusion upon us."

"The British, you say?" Missus James bent and retrieved her poker, and held her hand out to Nathaniel, her fingers waggling. "Let them come. They'll get no further than my front door. Hand me that back, boy."

"There's no need for that, Missus James," Nathaniel said, holding the knife out of her reach. "We'll be leaving before it comes to that, you and Anna and I and all of the others, remember? We had a meeting about it, and I recall that you were there."

"Oh, you may have had a meeting, but no Redcoat is going to chase me out of the home that Mister James built for me with his own two hands. I'll stay, and you can give me my knife now." Her eyes seemed to clear, and she glared at him, her hand still outstretched.

He laid the handle of the knife in her palm and her fingers closed over it.

"That's a good lad. Now, you two can stay here until the British have left, but if you want to watch them, the view is better from upstairs."

"Thank you kindly, Missus James," Nathaniel said, trying to recover his aplomb. He never expected an elderly widow to be the troublemaker for their plans to evacuate.

"Follow me," she said crisply, and led them to the kitchen,

where she set down her weapons, and then up the narrow stairs to the top floor.

The light up there was far better, as the shutters were all left somewhat ajar. This also made it easier to look out and see what was happening in the roads below.

Her voice quiet now, the widow said, "There they are, at the top of the bluff."

Nathaniel peered out past her, and saw the British general just a couple hundred feet distant, talking to an officer and gesturing again out toward the river. The other man seemed to be taking notes, his quill moving rapidly over a sheet of paper held on a handheld wooden writing-board.

The general was holding another page, and he consulted this now, looking around as though trying to get his bearings. He pointed to the road that led past the widow James' house, and the party moved in their direction.

Nathaniel started to tense up, and then was surprised to see the general approach the front of a house two doors down. He drew himself up and rapped at the front door, and a moment later, Captain Richards, the militia leader, answered, his musket clenched upright in his hand.

Several of the Redcoats accompanying the general leveled their guns on the man, but the general turned and waved them away. He and Captain Richards spoke for a few minutes, the conversation looking reasonably genial from what Nathaniel could see. Finally, the general bowed slightly and took his leave of the house, and the party returned to the road and marched together back to the road leading down the bluff.

After they had disappeared down the slope of the road,

Nathaniel stepped back from the window and looked at Anna and Missus James. "Will you two stay here while I go and find out from Captain Richards what the British had to say to him?"

Missus James looked like she was ready to argue with him, but Anna said, "Of course, Nathaniel. But hurry back so that you may tell us whether we need to start packing up."

"Or sharpening my knives," the widow said darkly, but she nodded, and Nathaniel made his way back downstairs.

He slipped out of the house and sprinted down to Captain Richards' place, knocking on the door urgently when he reached it. Captain Richards opened it immediately, his gun still in his hand, and a look of barely controlled rage on his face.

When he saw Nathaniel, his expression softened, but only a little. "Come in, Nathaniel. I was afraid you were someone else who had been guided to my very door by some spy in our community. However, I am glad that you have come, for General Cornwallis' comments bear directly on your assigned tasks."

"Cornwallis? That's not a name I've heard before. Who is he?"

"He did not explain himself, but said only that he and his engineer were here to consider how defensible the positions here at York-Town are, in comparison with their other options. He did not say as much, but I believe that he intends to take our town and fortify it as a British stronghold."

Chapter 20

A peal of thunder woke Nathaniel, and for a confused moment, he was back on the field at Waxhaws, cannon flashing and speaking in the dark while he waited to be relieved of his insensate and useless arm. The rattle of windowpanes in the wind of the storm was the jingle of the approaching cavalry, their sabers raised high into the night sky.

Then he was awake and rolling out of his bed to pull on his breeches. Over the crash of thunder and the wet drumbeat of rain on the roof of the house, he'd heard a pounding at the door.

Nathaniel opened the door a crack, and was surprised when a flash of lightning revealed Captain Richards, soaked to the skin, with a wild look in his eye.

"The British have been spotted coming up the river," he said. The flickering light of the storm continued to illuminate the doorway, and the grumble of distant thunder was punctuated now and again with nearer strokes.

Instantly fully awake, Nathaniel asked, "How many?"

"All of them, it would appear. They've already occupied Gloucester, across the river, and there can be no doubt that they mean to establish themselves here, as well. I'm ordering a general evacuation, not just you and your lot, but all of us who can be removed. York is a British town now."

Nathaniel took a deep breath. A small part of his mind

was grimly amused that he had come home for peace and to leave the war behind, but it had followed him right to his new bedroom. He dismissed the thought, though, replying crisply, "I will get my people together and have them collect their baggage."

"Leave nothing behind that you can help that might be of use to the enemy."

Nathaniel nodded, his mind already racing ahead to the tasks which must be completed before the sun rose, and those which must wait for the light of day. He reached out and grasped Captain Richards' upper arm for a moment. "May God be with you in the test we face today, my friend."

He released the militia commander's arm, and the other man replied before turning away into the storm, "May the great Author of the world smile upon you, as well, sir."

Nathaniel closed the door and went to go wake his Ma. On the way, he threw some more wood on the fire. There was no need to conserve it now, as whatever they did not use would warm British soldiers.

He rapped his knuckles on her door hard enough that he knew he'd feel it all day, calling through it, "Ma, we must fly. The British are coming."

He heard her groan, and then heard her footfalls padding softly to the door. She opened it and asked querulously, "Just like that? No fight, nor any resistance?"

"Captain Richards says that there are enough of them landed at Gloucester already that it appears that they mean to make a base for their operations right here. We might resist against a mere foraging party, but faced with their main army, we have no answer but flight."

She seemed to shrink before his eyes, and then she nodded. "What can I do?"

"Gather what we cannot lose," he said. "Shoes, any clothes that may serve, your kitchen goods, what foodstuffs we have. I must go and organize the wagons."

"Aye, you've your duty again, haven't you?" Her tone carried the faintest edge of accusation.

"I have, Ma. This is something that I can be useful at, and what I can do in the coming hours may make the difference between a safe retreat and a miserable captivity for us all."

"Go, then, but do not forget to attend to those who love you." She gave him a meaningful look, and Nathaniel thought immediately of Anna.

In the past fortnight, he had summoned the bravery to speak to her father, and the interview had gone as well as it could have, under the strained general circumstances. Mister Ware had pointed out that the moment was inauspicious, but said that he had no other objections, and so their betrothal was formalized, but no date was agreed upon just yet.

Still, Nathaniel felt a special responsibility to her, and handily, her father owned one of the wagons he needed now.

He donned his woolen coat and a knitted cap and pushed the front door open into a gust of wind from the storm.

Though the rekindled fire in the hearth had lit the kitchen up pretty well, the darkness outside was nearly impenetrable as the door banged shut behind him. His feet knew the way to Anna's house well enough, though, that he only needed the light of the now-infrequent flashes of lightning to navigate there.

He pounded on the front door to ensure he would be heard

over the storm, and in a moment, one of Anna's brothers opened it, his face registering suspicion as he recognized Nathaniel. "Why do you rouse our family in the dead of night? Can you not wait until morning to share whispers with my sister?"

Nathaniel scowled at his prospective brother-in-law and answered, "I am here to gather up the wagon your father has pledged to the evacuation, and to alert him and the rest of your family that we are all to remove ourselves from the town. The British are arriving in force, and we must give the place over to them."

Anna's brother snorted. "Well, that's what comes of a lot of men playing at soldier, I suppose."

Nathaniel could feel his blood rising, but mastered himself.

"I am not here to argue, Tyler. Wake the house and tell your father that I need the wagon and team as soon as he can bring them. We'll be going out the Williamsburg road, as the enemy is approaching from the river."

He turned and left, not trusting himself to wrangle with Anna's brother any longer.

The man had refused militia service, and he had often hinted that he thought things would be better after the British had defeated the rebellion. As he trudged off through the downpour to the next house on the road to spread the alert, Nathaniel wondered idly whether Tyler was actually a Tory, albeit one who lacked the courage even to declare himself for the Crown.

The storm continued to abate as Nathaniel went from door to door, and by the time the morning was starting to make itself known by a brightening of the sky in the direction of the river, he had completed his rounds and was waiting by the road out of town. The rain had stopped, and only a fitful breeze remained to remind him of the night's storm.

His ma came up the road, lugging her prized copper kettle, full of kitchen implements, and padded with all manner of clothing, both hers and Nathaniel's.

He hurried forward and reached out his hand to take the kettle from her.

"You should have left that for me to come gather, Ma."

She shrugged as she handed the copper over.

He nearly dropped it, as it was far heavier even than he had expected, and he exclaimed, "What do you have in here?"

"Couldn't see leaving behind the good cast iron," she said. "So I set it into the bottom of the copper, and stacked everything else up atop it."

He chuckled and adjusted his grip on the handle. "I am glad that you made it all fit. I will go and put it on the wagon."

He lugged the load over to the closest of the waiting wagons, and as he started to heave it up into the back, he lost his footing and went down into the mud. The last thing he remembered seeing was the copper kettle flying upward and then inevitably coming down toward him through the air.

Chapter 21

Nathaniel awoke with a groan, and tried to sit up. He was immobilized, though, by some unseen force, and he heard quick footsteps approaching on the wood floor. The wizened face of Missus James swam in his vision for a moment, and *tsk*ed to herself as he tried again to raise himself from the hard bed where he found himself.

"You stay still, child. You look to have stove in some ribs, and I've secured you to the bed to stop you hurting yourself any further. Your Anna is downstairs making up some plasters as I've instructed her."

The room was as dark as the last time he'd been in Missus James' house, and he could hear no sound from outside. Nathaniel lay back and breathed, pain lancing through his chest as he did so. He believed the old widow that he'd broken some ribs.

He remembered what he'd been doing, then, and croaked out, "The British?"

"Aye, they're here, and most everyone from the town has gone. Your mother wanted to stay and tend to you, but your pa made her leave with him. Since I wasn't going anywhere, they left you with me. And, of course, your young woman insisted on staying with you, too. Made quite a scene, she did."

Nathaniel took another pained breath. "Where did our people go?"

Missus James shrugged. "I didn't take note of it, as I was not accompanying them. They were following Mister Richards up the road toward Williamsburg when they took their leave of me, but I know not whether they will find any refuge there."

There was a small sound at the door to the room, and Nathaniel tried to roll over to see. He was brought up short by a pain intense enough that it brought stars to his closed eyes, and he cried aloud.

"I told you I'd secured you to keep you from hurting yourself further, boy. That didn't mean that I intended for you to try your restraints. Come in, child, and bring those plasters here."

As he opened his eyes a crack, unsurprised to find that they were welling up with involuntary tears at the pain, Anna swam into view, her expression one of grave concern, and her own eyes red from crying.

Nathaniel closed his eyes again and mumbled, "I am sorry for causing so much trouble and concern. I should have been watching my footing better."

"What you should have done was to let your ma carry that load, instead of pretending that you are equal to every task that any other man can do." Missus James' tone was crisp, but it softened as she added, "Watched the whole thing, I did. You're to be commended for trying to help your ma, but you've got to know your limits, boy."

Anna walked over and took his hand, saying quietly but firmly, "Your strengths lie in other places than do most men's, Nathaniel. There's no need to try to prove yourself the equal of someone like Michael Bell."

In a flash, Nathaniel remembered that that was the name of

the tobacco farmer's son to whom Anna had once been promised. "You once thought well enough of Michael Bell," he said, and it pained him to hear the peevish tone in his own voice.

Anna flushed red, but said steadily, "My father thought well of Patrick Bell, Michael's father. Michael and I were never more than childhood friends, whose fathers made an arrangement that we never agreed to. I never had any interest in anyone but you, Nathaniel."

Missus James raised her eyebrows and turned to leave the room, while Anna looked Nathaniel in the eye, her gaze unwavering.

For his part, it was Nathaniel's turn to blush, and he stammered, "I-I never knew."

"Because I never told you, until you came back from the war. You thought that everything had changed, and that you were less of a man than you had departed as, but I still saw the same man I knew, the same man I'd grown up admiring and wishing that I only had leave to share my thoughts with."

She brushed her hair back from her face where it had fallen as she spoke, and Nathaniel could see that her eyes were again brimming with tears. "I happened to meet you on the road, and I could see that you were still the same modest, devoted son to your parents as I had known before, but more than that, you were now covered in glory for your dedication to the cause of our freedom—and you couldn't even see it."

She motioned at his stump. "You gave of your very body to fight against the Crown, and then made your way home, thinking nothing of the effort that voyage represented. A man who could do that ought hold his head high in any company, yet you seemed to think that you should be ashamed of your sacrifice."

She gestured at the angry red scrape on his side, where his Ma's kettle had landed on him. "And now you've gone and hurt yourself more, trying to prove that you're the equal of someone like Michael Bell. Well, you are not his equal. You are far better than him and his Tory family, fighting on the other side, against independence."

She threw her hands into the air in a frustrated motion. "To tell the truth, I was relieved when I heard the news that he had joined a Loyalist militia, because I knew that my father would release me from the match with a Tory, but I was terrified that Michael would come face-to-face with you by some chance, and that one of you would die somehow in the transaction."

Nathaniel drew a deep, painful breath, and said, "Truly, I am glad to know all of this. It explains much that haunted me, and makes me all the more certain that I want to spend my life with you."

He winced as he inhaled, but he continued, "That day on the hill, I could make no sense of your interest in speaking to me, but I welcomed it all the same. When you made your interest in me known even more clearly, I confess that I wondered whether you were having sport at my expense, as I could not otherwise make sense of a girl with your qualities wanting to be courted by someone with such limited prospects to offer."

She started to object, and he said quickly, "Let me finish. I am aware that my prospects are limited to some sort of work that does not involve most forms of labor, as there is little that can be done with just one hand."

He took another wincing breath. "My first attempts to

learn a trade that I could do with just one hand, and with the tools of my mind, were not particularly auspicious. Meeting you, though, gave me cause to redouble my efforts, and I have every faith that once this affair is concluded, I will be able to practice some form of useful arts, whether with ciphers or something else that I have not yet hit upon."

She nodded soberly and said, "I am glad that I was able to influence you to find your way through the hard work required to learn a useful trade."

"Are you two twittering birds done cooing at one another? We need to get that plaster on you, boy." Missus James' tone belied her harsh words, though, as she sounded genuinely happy for the first time since they'd met her.

Anna smiled and beckoned her in. Missus James showed the younger woman how to apply the plaster, spreading it over Nathaniel's ribs as he hissed in pain at the contact. After they had stopped touching him, though, the cool weight of the plaster, plus whatever the widow had instructed Anna to put in it, seemed to be relieving his pain somewhat.

He lay back and in just a few minutes, was drifting off to sleep. It was not a restful sleep, as every breath still brought fresh agonies, and movement was, of course, still impossible, but it was some sleep. He was dimly aware of the women moving around the house as he slumbered, and once, he half woke up at the aroma of food, but he was already asleep again when Anna brought a bowl of stew up for him.

When he next awoke, she was sitting in a wooden chair beside his bed, her head lolling back in sleep. The position must have been anything but comfortable, Nathaniel thought, but he found that he quite enjoyed hearing her snore lightly. The rise and fall of her shoulders as she breathed gave him a pattern to mimic in his own breathing, and he practiced just pacing her for a while.

In the process, he must have fallen asleep again, for the next time he opened his eyes, both Anna and Missus James were peering anxiously out through the window in his room. He summoned the breath to call over to them, "What is the matter?"

Anna was the first to answer. "The British are searching and looting each house on this road and will be here soon. I have convinced Missus James to let me do the talking, and that we will explain to the troops when they come that we are here for your convalescence, and will make no trouble for them. Of course, should they prove to be too persistent about insisting on taking what they want, Missus James will have her poker and her knives close to hand."

"Won't be afraid to use them, either. Mister James and I lived out at the frontier for a piece, and I had to defend our house against the Indians on several occasions. They soon enough learned to give my house a wide berth when they were out raiding."

Despite himself, Nathaniel smiled. He had no doubt that Missus James had proven capable of discouraging any who had been foolish enough to test her, and the knowledge that she had faced such difficulties explained a lot about the sort of person she appeared to be now.

He wondered idly whether Mister James had been possessed of so forceful a personality as his widow, or whether she had run roughshod over him in their marriage. That then led him to ponder what sort of marriage he and Anna would have, when the time came.

In the midst of this happy consideration, he heard both women gasp simultaneously.

"What is it? I would come to the window myself and spy alongside you, but I am a little occupied at present."

Anna tore herself away from the window and said in a low voice, "The soldiers have turned away from this road, and gone back down the bluff. It would appear that they are setting afire the warehouses below town."

Chapter 22

"How does this feel, boy?" The widow's hands were not particularly gentle as they moved over his still-tender ribs, but for the first time since he'd hurt himself, he was not driven to wince or cry out as she checked his progress.

"Tolerable," he said. "Anna's plasters seem to have done some good."

The older woman snorted. "Binding you to the bed most of the time did you more good, I'll wager, as it prevented you from doing yourself greater harm." She waved a hand dismissively. "In any event, you are probably healed up enough now to stir about out of doors, although there is little worth seeing except Redcoats and the works they are throwing up all about town. I don't expect that they would appreciate you poking about those, either."

"As much as I might like to bring some intelligence to our forces should the opportunity present itself, I rather doubt that the British will make it all that easy. I should like to venture down to my pa's warehouse and see whether it yet stands."

"Is there aught you can do about it if it does not?"

"Well . . . not really, no."

"And if it does stand, they aren't going to let you inside. They've seized up all of the useful goods that they could find in town already, and have brought back all manner of goods that they collected from the surrounding area, as well. There can be no doubt that everything within their reach is forfeit to their needs."

He sighed. "In truth, our own armies operate in much the same manner, when the opportunity arises. We rarely received any supplies provided by the Congress, and even when we were able to pay for what we needed, it was only in Continentals, which are hardly worth the paper on which they're printed."

The widow favored him with a sour look. "Too well I know, boy. We've seen other townsfolk who remained moving about, so if you should like to take a turn about the town, I am certain that Anna would like to get out of the house, as well. I've kept her out of sight, as even the most well-supervised troops may forget their manners in the presence of an unaccompanied young woman, particularly one as well-formed as your Anna."

It was Nathaniel's turn to snort derisively. "In my experience, these troops are anything but well-mannered when it comes to colonial women. They regard them as just another commodity to be seized as desired and cast aside when they've finished with them. While I am glad for Anna's company and her assistance in my healing, I would have been less anxious were she out of their reach."

Missus James nodded. "Well, what can't be helped, can be endured. I'll go and fetch you one of Mister James' shirts, as your own was much stained and torn when you were injured."

She went down the stairs, and Nathaniel stood up experimentally. His legs felt weak after a fortnight of confinement, and his head was a little light, as well. He had only been upright in the past two weeks to attend to the call of nature, and then only for a few moments at a time before he suffered to be returned to a prone position in the bed. While he did not enjoy the process, he could hardly argue with the benefits he had reaped as a result of the widow's firmness with him.

Taking a deep breath, he only felt a ghost of the crushing pain that had reduced him to tears on more than one occasion during his convalescence. He walked over to the window to look out and see what he could of the town.

From the window he had chosen, he could see the river, crowded with British ships. Smaller boats shuttled back and forth between the ships and both sides of the river, and it seemed to his inexpert eye that the ships were arrayed in a haphazard manner, perhaps wherever their anchors could find purchase in the bottom of the river.

He heard a small noise behind him, and he turned to find Anna standing there with a shirt.

She smiled at him shyly and held it out to him. "I took the liberty, with Missus James' permission, naturally, of altering this one for your arm."

Nathaniel smiled gratefully at her and turned the shirt about in his hand, finding the bottom of it to put his head through. He'd become quite adept at pulling on a shirt on one-handed, but this time, his sore ribs limited his ability to turn and wriggle into the garment.

After a couple of tries, he found himself all tangled in it, until he finally stopped struggling with the twisted fabric and said meekly, "Help me, please?"

He could hear Anna giggling lightly, and felt her small, quick hands pulling at the cloth this way and then that, until she was able to work the neck of the shirt over his head. Her face was close by his, her eyes dancing in mirth, and she darted forward to give him a quick kiss on the cheek.

"I wish you were less stubborn about getting help with the things that are difficult for you." She smiled as she stepped back and held the sleeve for his good arm out straight so he could slip his hand into it.

"I asked for help, didn't I?" Nathaniel felt a bit mulish in the face of her gentle scolding, and he could hear that his tone was sharp, too. "I'm sorry. I dislike running into my limitations, particularly where others can see it happening."

She answered quietly and seriously, "I know, Nathaniel. I didn't mean to laugh at you, but if you had seen yourself, I doubt that you could have stopped a chuckle or two."

He smiled at her. "I suppose I did look a sight, at that."

From the doorway to the room, Missus James said, "You looked as though you were engaged in a mortal struggle with the shirt, and the shirt was getting the better of you. If you can't laugh at yourself when you're doing something like that, you'll never be able to cope with the day when you need to untie a knot in order to free yourself."

Nathaniel turned to her as he pulled the shirt straight where it was still bunched up and twisted. "I fear that learning to do that may be a longer task than was healing from my injuries."

She nodded. "It will go faster if you can listen to your Anna's laughter and join in, rather than getting your back up."

She turned to leave, and Nathaniel called after her, "Thank you for the shirt, Missus James. And for the advice. I shall endeavor to make good use of them both."

The old woman nodded without turning around and

continued down the stairs.

Nathaniel looked back at Anna to find her with a skeptical little smile on her face.

"You'll try, I am certain," she said. "But without someone reminding you, I have a feeling that you would quickly come to disregard both the advice and the quality of the shirt. You are fortunate indeed that I will be happy to remind you."

She grinned, and Nathaniel couldn't help but grin back.

He shrugged and replied, "I am grateful for that, my dear friend. Perhaps you can also remind me from time to time that I was no paragon of grace even with two arms, and so I should not attempt activities that would have been demanding for me even before this happened." He motioned to his missing arm.

She made a conciliatory gesture and said, "I will remind you of how very capable you are, and that the evidence of your capacity for great things stands before you. Now, should you like to demonstrate to the enemies of our country that no mere amputation can stop an American from venturing forth in his hometown, even when a whole army stands in his way?"

She extended her arm, and he tucked his hand into the crook of her elbow, following her to the stairs. They had to disengage in order to descend, but she put her arm back out for him once they were on the ground floor.

Outside, their lighthearted mood disappeared quickly, and they shot each other bleak expressions as they saw the changes that had been wrought upon their little town in the course of just a few short days.

Many of the houses stood with their doors ajar, clearly having been ransacked for anything useful. Items that had been pulled out into the light for closer examination, only to be cast aside, littered the road. Almost as soon as they left the widow's house, Nathaniel could see a pile of chairs smashed to kindling, broken dishes, a shapeless pile of clothing, and some old account books, and he felt Anna's hand grip his arm more tightly.

She said in almost a whisper, "I don't think I want to see what they've done to my father's house. My family had to leave so much behind . . . "

Nathaniel didn't want to see what the occupiers had done to his ma's house, but he would need to go anyway. Despite the injury it had done him, he was glad that she'd gotten her prized copper and the most important of her kitchen implements out. Still, there had been treasured furniture and more clothing than she could carry away, not to mention small things like the new bowls they'd eaten from together each morning.

They continued down the street, noting that the stripping of houses had passed by a few homes, including a couple which Nathaniel had suspected might belong to secret Tories. Some of those looked to still be occupied—though in fairness, Nathaniel had to admit that Missus James was no Tory, yet her house was occupied and had not been violated.

They rounded a corner and found themselves practically face-to-face with a patrol of four Redcoats. The two in front immediately lifted their muskets, training them on the couple.

One of the British soldiers behind the pair who menaced Nathaniel and Anna with their guns said briskly, "Who are you two, and why are you wandering the town?"

Anna held her head high and answered, "We are guests of the widow James, whose house your men inspected on your arrival here. This man was hurt in the evacuation of the town, and she and I were tending to his wounds."

The British soldier peered more closely at Nathaniel and nodded with comprehension. "Yes, yes, I remember hearing about you. You are, as I recall, a paroled casualty of earlier action?"

"Aye, that I am," Nathaniel answered tightly.

The soldier nodded. "I will remind you, then, that your parole extends to the act of supplying to the rebel forces information about the disposition of forces and the defenses laid out in this place. You are free to go about your business, so long as you can abide by that constraint."

"I can do that readily enough. All that I had in mind to do, other than getting some air after my confinement, was to survey my family's property and see how it fares under your army's custody."

The soldier pursed his lips thoughtfully. "Do not think to interfere in the usage of your property for military purposes, nor in the seizure of lawful spoils of war. Mind, too, that you do not get in the way of men performing their duties as they establish this place with the proper defenses and all that is necessary to house themselves."

Nathaniel frowned, but said, "I will not interfere in whatever your forces here think is proper, so long as none threatens harm to my person or that of my betrothed."

The British soldier bowed toward Anna. "Neither of you should have anything to worry about during our stay here."

Nathaniel did not respond directly, but returned the man's bow, unsmiling, and then led Anna by the hand around the squad, continuing down the road toward the bluff. For their part, the British soldiers re-formed into a patrol and marched off in the opposite direction.

As soon as they were out of earshot, Nathaniel said to Anna, "Well, I suppose I should go and see what has become of my family's property, having said that I would do so. I confess that I am curious as to whether they fired my father's warehouse on their arrival, when it looked to you and Missus James as though they were burning the buildings down there."

Anna squeezed his hand. "I could not tell which warehouses they were putting to the torch, only that there were prodigious flames leaping up from below the bluff, in that direction."

As they walked toward the road that cut through the bluff and led to the docks, Nathaniel commented, "I cannot think of why they should have fired any of the structures down there, when they could have instead turned them to their own uses."

Anna shrugged. "They may have wanted to send a message to some of the residents of this town, or simply avenge themselves against property whose defenders were unable to protect it."

"You may be right," Nathaniel said, as they turned the corner to where they could finally see some of the lower part of town.

The homes and warehouses nearest to the road seemed to be intact, and everywhere there seemed to be masses of soldiers moving about, including a long column of men carrying goods up from the docks.

Wagon after wagon streamed by, laden with everything from folded canvas for a city's worth of tents, to barrels upon barrels stamped with markings that were anywhere from merely obscure to completely impenetrable. Between the wagons were formations of men, their officers calling out maneuvers and orders as they went.

Anna and Nathaniel watched the procession for some time, neither of them saying anything. The road down to the lower part of town was completely full of men and wagons coming up from the ships, and there was no space for them to even pass that way themselves.

One of the officers paused and called out to them, "You've no need to go into the lower town. That area is reserved to His Majesty's forces alone, and any property that you may hold there is subject to this army's needs."

Nathaniel waved with his good arm. "Aye, and we won't attempt it. We were only curious as to what is happening in our town."

"Mind that you do not attempt any spying, either, sir," the officer said, and then had to hurry to catch up with his troops.

Nathaniel muttered imprecations under his breath, but stood for a while longer with Anna, watching.

Finally, Anna said in a low voice, "It appears as though the entire British army on these shores has come here to fight."

Nathaniel replied just as quietly, "I only wonder if the American army will come to meet them on the field of battle here."

Chapter 23

The sound of distant thunder rolled over the town in the warmth of the summer morning. Nathaniel scowled and scanned the skies, finding no clouds visible. He sat back from the garden plot where the widow James had set him to pulling out weeds and looking for pests on her potatoes.

While it was well that he was developing another useful skill, with his education as a clerk interrupted, he did not love the repetitive and uninteresting work of identifying and destroying that which did not belong in the garden. However, the work was necessary, he knew.

With the army staking first claim on any goods that were available in the area—and even going out on foraging parties to find anything that residents might have squirreled away for their own needs—it became necessary for all of those who remained in town to provide for themselves as best they could.

There was no beef or mutton to be had at all, and even most of the chickens that had wandered the roads of town after the departure of its residents had long since disappeared into British stew pots. While some of the remaining York-Town residents had established themselves on friendly terms with the occupying soldiers, and had so been able to wheedle occasional meat for their tables, Nathaniel, Anna, and Missus James were united in their determination to remain self-sufficient.

One who had established very friendly relations with the British soldiers was Anna's brother Tyler. After giving up on inspecting the warehouse abandoned by Nathaniel's pa, Anna and Nathaniel had given in to the temptation to see how her house fared, they'd been surprised to find her brother taking his ease on the front porch.

He scowled as he saw their approach, and called out, "Weren't you supposed to be organizing the withdrawal of the women, children, and other feeble?"

Nathaniel gritted his teeth at the man's implication, but answered evenly, "I was injured in the course of the evacuation, and your sister stayed to help care for me. What has you staying in town, when most have sought safety in Williamsburg or Richmond?"

"Oh, I thought that someone ought to stay and keep watch over our house. We have more to lose than some in town, and I wanted to ensure that our guests would not mistake our house for one belonging to rebels."

Anna tensed up beside Nathaniel, and she said coldly, "Do you mean to say that you have cast your lot in with our oppressors? I knew that you were self-dealing, Tyler, but I had no idea that you were a devotee of Benedict Arnold and his treason against our cause."

Tyler smiled at her insolently. "Oh, my poor, simple sister. Don't you understand where our family's interests lie? Our father is a landowner and farmer, and this rebellion will never serve to advance his hopes for our improvement as well as did the benevolent and wise rule of our sovereign. This whole sorry affair will be concluded in after not much longer, and when that day comes, you will be glad that someone from our family had the foresight to declare openly for the right side of the contest."

Anna did not reply, but turned her back on her brother and the house where she had grown up, saying to Nathaniel, "We have other matters to attend to yet today, and I see no further need to pass any time here."

As they'd walked away, Anna's head had been held high and proud, but once they were out of sight of her home, she'd thrown herself into Nathaniel's arms and sobbed. After she pulled herself together, she never mentioned her brother to him again, nor did she ever venture down the street where her home stood.

In his darker moments, Nathaniel wondered if Tyler hadn't been right to have provided for himself by changing sides—if he had ever truly been on the American side at all—and those thoughts crept in most often when he was engaged in the hard work of ensuring that he and the women had enough to eat.

Now, as he stood up from the potato patch and rubbed the dirt from his hand off on the filthy left leg of his breeches, he heard another rolling ripple of thunder, and realized that it must be distant cannon from somewhere.

Glancing over at the fine brick house up the road from the James' place—which had been taken over by the British officers in command of the town—he saw a young soldier approaching at a mad dash. Nathaniel smiled grimly and headed back inside Missus James' house. He could ask for no better confirmation that there was something afoot.

Closing the door behind himself, he called out, "Have we enough water in the house? It sounds as though there is the possibility of action soon."

As he anticipated, this announcement brought both women

scurrying away from the tasks that had occupied them. Anna came in from the dining room, where she had been darning socks, and the widow James came through the other side of the front hall, wiping her hands off on her apron.

"What is this, now? What makes you think that?" As usual, the older woman's tone was brusque and businesslike.

Nathaniel shrugged. "I heard what I took to be cannon fire, and then I saw a messenger arriving at the headquarters building with the greatest of dispatch. The only conclusion I could reasonably draw was that he was there to deliver word of some hostile force approaching."

He gestured around the house. "If that is the case, then we need to be certain that the preparations we've discussed are in readiness. I should very much like to avoid being hurt by our friends, or used by the enemy to keep our friends at bay."

Missus James nodded. "I'll go down to the basement and check the water, but so long as the casks have held tight, we should be well-supplied. We are short on foodstuffs, but that's nothing new. Pity they couldn't wait until we had time to harvest everything from the garden, but we have some put by."

Anna said with a half-smile, "The British soldiers will never think to look for it under the pile of old clothes I set atop the barrels, so it should be secure, should they come around looking for forage again."

Nathaniel smiled back at her. "The sense I've gotten from the British soldiers who've been incautious enough to comment on the matter is that they have foraged pretty widely around the area, and are starting to run out of plantations and farms to raid. They'll have to start bringing in supplies from elsewhere . . . although, if the American forces are close enough for cannon to be audible, they may have missed their opportunity to do so."

"Well, if you happen to see a chicken about, this would be a capital time to bring it in. If it's a hen, we can keep it quiet in the cellar and use its eggs. Otherwise . . . "

The older woman grinned at him, and Nathaniel said, "Soup would be a nice addition to our diet. The meal and wheat I was able to bring back from where my ma had hidden it in our house is nearly spent, and the potatoes aren't quite big enough to bring in yet."

"Oh, they're probably worth bringing in, if we're to be confined within the house." The widow wrapped her arms around herself, and rubbed one arm with her hand as though she were cold—despite the summer heat.

"Until we know there will be action, should we not let them grow as large as they can?"

"You're right, of course, lad. I just remember being trapped inside a blockhouse at the frontier one summer when the Cherokee were on the warpath, and we lost an entire crop to their raids. There was good food ready to harvest in the fields, but we listened to the counsel of someone there who said that they were just passing through. We got very hungry indeed that year."

Nathaniel nodded. "I am sensible of your concerns, but I think that we'll have a little more notice of the immediacy of our need."

As he spoke, they could hear a ruckus from the street outside, and all three of them rushed to the window to see what they could of the source of the noise. A column of soldiers was marching past on the main road, just visible from the house, at a quick-march pace that they'd not observed in the occupiers up to this time.

Horses drew a cannon on its carriage, urged on by an officer whose face was nearly as red as his jacket.

His eyebrows raised, Nathaniel turned and looked at the two women. "It would appear that they are in a hurry, and it looks as though they are concerned about a threat from above town, rather than from the river. I should like to peer out from upstairs and see whether there is anything visible that might explain their hurry."

"Mind that you do not appear to be acting the spy," Missus James said.

"Oh, I've no doubt that the Continentals have plenty of spies abroad in these parts already. I can add nothing to their knowledge, only to our own."

"Very well," the old woman said. "I'll keep watch on the road from down here."

"I'll come with you," Anna told Nathaniel, slipping her hand into his.

He gave it a small, grateful squeeze and together, they made their way up the stairs and to the window that faced in the direction that the British forces had been headed. What they could see past the other houses was only that the Redcoats seemed to be quickly throwing up a series of defensive positions around the town.

"Would you look at how many soldiers there are out there?" Nathaniel drew Anna close, feeling somehow that she was safer from the massed men laboring in the fields outside of town if she was in his embrace.

Further out into the fields and into the woods beyond, though, Nathaniel could see no sign of the American forces, nor anything that explained the sound of cannon, so he led Anna over to the other side of the room, to the window that looked out over the river and up the bay toward the ocean.

There, he saw a sight that made his heart leap with excitement. Two huge warships were at anchor, just visible in the distance, accompanied by a smaller ship, and although he could not make out any colors at their range, he could see that the British ships in the river between York-Town and Gloucester on the other side were swarming with activity.

Launches pulled away from them in a steady stream, heavily loaded down with men and armaments—Nathaniel thought he could see cannon, as well as barrel upon barrel that he suspected was filled with gunpowder, based on how carefully they were handled as men labored to unload them upon the quay.

Anna asked wonderingly, "What has them all so stirred up?"

"Oh, did you not see the ships further out there? They're not easy to spot, but they appear to be what our naval friends call 'ships of the line.' As I was given to understand it, that means that they form the primary portion of a line of battle in a naval engagement."

Anna gripped Nathaniel's upper arm and looked over his shoulder where he was pointing, her breath tickling his ear as she leaned in close to him.

Suddenly aware of how closely she was pressed against him, he willed himself to remain still, and merely indicated where he'd seen the strange ships.

"There and there. Notice how high they stand up from the water. You see how the British ships here have but one row of cannon? Those have several, in one layer stacked over the other. I can only imagine that it must be the most awful sound you could ever hope to hear, should they all fire at once."

"Aye, I see them," she said quietly. "Are you so sure that they are friendly to us?"

He turned to grin at her, and she stepped back, which both relieved and disappointed him. However, he focused on answering her question.

"These fellows seem to think so." He gestured at the activity on the ships in the river.

Tipping his head in the direction of the first window they'd looked through, he added, "As do those men. I'd say that we are sitting between two great rocks in a flood, and they are about to strike together right over our heads."

Chapter 24

Nathaniel hurried down the road, his heart fairly skipping with joy. He was careful to keep an expression of grim neutrality on his face as he went, but it took real effort.

He'd ventured out of the house to see whether he could secure any food or news from the occupiers, and although nobody had proven willing to part with what they had taken as fair spoils from the surrounding countryside, one soldier with whom he'd previously had relatively friendly discussions had let an exciting tidbit of news slip, and Nathaniel was bursting to share it with Anna and the widow James.

He opened the door to the house, slipping inside, and as soon as it was secured behind him, he called out, "Anna! Missus James! I've intelligence of what is afoot beyond our town." He continued into the kitchen, where both women were busy bagging up the potatoes that he'd finally dug up after considering and discussing the matter with Missus James.

The potatoes had spent a day drying in the sun after he'd dug them out, and then all three of them had ventured out to get water and wash their harvest. Another day in the sun to dry, and they were ready to store up. There were enough of them to last all winter if there was other food available, and enough to keep their bellies filled for at least a couple of months otherwise.

Not looking up from where she was delicately setting layer

upon layer of potatoes into the hempen bags laid out on the table, the widow asked, "What has you so worked up, lad?"

"General Lafayette and his American army are on their way here. He's been seen at Williamsburg, and the British forces are falling back in anticipation of a siege here. There are other forces afield in that direction, as well, and the soldier I spoke with said that between those forces advancing over land, and the ships in the bay by sea—which are French, by the way, and reinforced by a great fleet further out—there is a very real fear that their position here may be overrun by the Americans and their allies."

Anna regarded him with wide eyes. "Is that really cause for celebration? After all, if those two rocks you spoke of a few days ago collide together over our little town, what hope have we of surviving the sparks they may strike?"

Nathaniel gave her what he hoped was a comforting smile. "We have but to observe their approach, and then ensure we keep our heads low when they are actually engaging with one another."

He thought back to his own experience of a hard-fought action.

"When the day was done at Waxhaws, there was still town enough to bring in the hurt, and see to the dead. If our troops overcome the British here, it will not likely be by having so many more men or guns than the enemy, but by being able to out-wait them, and hem them in without resupply. So long as our side can still get supplies, while denying the British access to food and powder, the conclusion will be foregone."

"It's a pretty picture you paint, boy, but even I can see two fatal flaws in your theory." Missus James held up her index finger. "One: we remain here and share the fate of the British forces, including their starvation, should it come to that." She held up a second finger beside the first. "Two: the British are unlikely to tolerate a blockade by sea for very long, and their naval forces have a fearsome reputation, as I understand it."

She sat back and brushed her hands onto her skirt absently, as though they were covered in dirt. "As soon as they can call down a fleet from New-York, or send one up from Bermuda, they will drive a hole through the French fleet, and have anything they need delivered right up to the docks here at York-Town."

Nathaniel made a gesture of acknowledgment with his hand. "You may very well have the right of it, Missus James. But the soldier with whom I spoke seemed genuinely concerned, and his concern was transmitted from the highest levels of the army here by the usual means of rumor and whispers that bedevils every military operation in this country."

"Well, then, it sounds as though we had best get these potatoes put up and out of sight. A hungry army hemmed in among us will not scruple to leave us with anything at all to eat, should their own need grow sharp enough."

Once they finished with the chore, concealing the bags of potatoes behind a loose wall of boards in the cellar, Nathaniel seized upon another excuse to go out and learn what he could of the situation from the British outpost that had taken over the town.

"I remember that my ma put some of her clothing up in the rafters of her bedroom for storage, and I suspect that you two might be able to make use of some of it."

"Use caution," Anna said. "We already know that they suspect spies in their midst, so give them no reason to believe that you might be the source of the intelligence on which Lafayette is making his plans."

He smiled at her and gathered her into a one-armed embrace. "I shall take no untoward chances," he assured her. "I have in my favor the fact that I am well known to be complying with the command that I am not to have any communication outside of the town, nor to leave for any reason."

He released her and held her at arm's length, his hand on her shoulder. "I shan't be gone for long. I'm just looking to see if those clothes are still there, and then I'm coming straight back here."

The widow James looked over at him with a sour expression. "Don't think that your wounds will give you immunity to suspicion. You were fortunate that first day that the patrol you two encountered had been told of your presence in the town. There are many more soldiers about now, and they are more likely to see you as an object for sport than the honest townsperson you're claiming to be."

"Aye, I know, Missus James. I'll be careful."

She gave a little impatient huff and waved her hand as he left. "You'll do what you want to do, and I know it."

He didn't stay to argue with her, but instead, slipped out the front door of her house and hurried down the road toward his own.

As he approached his ma's house, he was shocked to see that the new bedroom that had just been added for him was half-disassembled, with all of the planking on the exterior pried away, and much of the wood within removed as well.

It looked like the only reason that more wasn't gone was that the roof over the addition was sagging dangerously, after one too many supporting beams had been pulled out of the wall.

He stared aghast at the seemingly random destruction, until a squad of British soldiers came swinging down the road toward the house. He hurried to get out of view, and then watched as their sergeant directed the men to continue pulling down the house.

"The siding first, men, as that's good material for walkways behind the earthworks. We need to get those heavier beams from the new section of the house, too, to shore up the wall."

A flash of anger passed over Nathaniel as he realized that the house where he'd spent his childhood with his ma was being converted into a machine of war against his own side. Worse, as they tore apart the house, they were singing a rough song about the joys of defeated men's wives and daughters that made him blush when he caught the repeated lyric.

More than at any moment since he'd been struck down on the field of battle, Nathaniel wished that he again had a musket, and could silence these depraved men and bring their work of deconstruction to an end.

However, he would never use a musket again, and even if he could, they were many and he was but one man. His heart burning with rage, he turned away to return to Missus James' house. As he went, he noticed that a few other houses around town had already been obliterated, their hearths standing alone, as though a great fire had passed through.

The fact that the agent of ruin that had leveled the homes of his neighbors, and now his own, was not the comparatively clean one of fire, but instead the filthy hands of coarse and laughing men, made it somehow all the worse.

Fire was at least impartial in its work. As he walked,

Nathaniel could see that the buildings that had been chosen for dismantling were all those of the men who had joined the militia, or supplied the Continental Army, or had otherwise supported the cause of independence. This was as personal as a knife to the gut, and by the time he reached Missus James' house, his vision was blurred by unshed tears.

He entered quietly and went up to his room, where he sat on the edge of his bed, staring at his good hand and wondering why this particular loss felt so horrible in comparison with all the others he'd suffered.

Anna came upstairs and sat beside him. His words tumbled out in a rush, unbidden and unstoppable.

"They are punishing the patriots in town by pulling down our houses and using them as raw lumber for the construction of their breastworks and platforms, from which they may well direct their fire upon the very owners of the former homes so reduced."

She said nothing, but only wrapped her arm around him, laying her head on his shoulder as the tears that he had kept at bay since the arrival of the British in town now seemed to all seek escape.

All of the sacrifice, all of the toil, seemed suddenly likely to come to nothing. The widow James was right—there was a vanishingly small likelihood that the Royal Navy would be blocked from resupplying this place for very long. Nathaniel knew all too well the disarray and poor condition of the American forces, and seeing the relative discipline and confidence of the regiments that occupied York-Town drove home the disparity between the two.

The French were useful allies, it was true, but how reliable would they be in the face of entrenched and well-drilled British forces in the countryside surrounding the town, never mind those on the seas, who had a long history of confounding the French? How long would it take them to conclude that the American cause was hopeless, and that their interests were better served in undermining English influence somewhere else in the world?

As his tears subsided and he felt the even, steady cycle of Anna's breathing beside him, Nathaniel wondered how long that would remain to him, and whether she would be taken from him by despair or disgust. He could see no way out of the darkness that gathered around the house as night fell, or around the town as the British closed their lines in preparation for whatever the Americans might try.

Chapter 25

The news struck Nathaniel like the first ray of sunlight bursting out from behind a storm cloud. It was all he could do to keep his reaction off his face and do no more than nod thoughtfully to his interlocutor, a slump-shouldered private of the occupying army.

"After we heard the cannonade, we were hopeful of relief by our friends in the navy, but instead, we received the news that our relief had fought against the French fleet, resulting in the loss of two frigates."

He sighed heavily. "What remains of our fleet has returned to sea, and even now if you look out at the river, you can see where we are scuttling our own troop ships in order to form a barrier against the French, or, God help us, the Americans joining their allies here to press an attack from the water."

The private shook his head sadly, adding, "What is worse is that there are rumors, too, that the American army has joined with Lafayette's forces at Williamsburg, and that Washington himself has taken command of the combined army. We are trapped here on this little spit of earth, with the French menacing us from the sea, and the Americans coming by land."

Nathaniel felt that decency demanded that he give the other man some sympathetic response, despite the soaring joy he felt in his own heart. "There is, at least, some room for maneuvers in the countryside around the town. Can you not march out and bring the fight to General Washington?"

"Aye, you would think so, wouldn't you? But our generals seem to have placed all of their hopes on their friends in the admiralty being able to break the French cordon, and so we are instead building defensive walls close about the town, and setting up our guns to hold those positions. I know that many of the men would prefer to haul the guns out to Williamsburg itself, but we are not granted the epaulettes to command this, so here we stay and wait."

"I thank you for giving me warning," Nathaniel said quite sincerely. "I should go back to my house and ensure that all is in readiness for whatever may happen next."

"Aye, that you should, for once the action starts, there will be none but yourself to keep you safe."

Nathaniel gave the talkative private a farewell wave and departed his company, keeping his step as steady as he could.

For a conversation that had started by Nathaniel inquiring about the availability of firewood now that access to the surrounding woods was cut off by the fortifications that had risen about the town, it had turned out to have provided something much more valuable than fuel for the hearth—for the first time in a fortnight, Nathaniel dared to hope.

Inside the house, the widow James was teaching Anna the finer points of darning socks when Nathaniel closed the door behind himself, finally permitting his grin to burst forth on his face. He leaned back against the door for a moment to gather himself, listening to the two women converse in the next room.

"A well-mended sock is probably stronger than it was when

it first came off your needles," Missus James said to Anna.

The younger woman giggled lightly. "This one is pretty strong already. Will that smell never come out of the yarn?"

The widow chuckled in reply, and Nathaniel pushed himself off the door to enter the room.

Missus James swiveled her head to turn and look at Nathaniel, frowning at his empty arm. "No wood to be had, I take it? We had better hope that this affair is concluded before the winter gets a proper start, never mind learning how to cook without fire."

"It is interesting that you bring up the affair here winding up," Nathaniel replied, seating himself across from the two women. He recounted what the British private had told him, adding, "So, you see, it does sound as though the British stratagem of trying to establish themselves here in York-Town is going to come to its crisis soon enough."

"That is wonderful news, Nathaniel!" Anna set aside her darning and jumped up to throw her arms around him. "Was there any talk of retreat in what he could tell you?"

"Nay," he answered. "It sounded as though their only potential avenue for retreat has been cut off by the French fleet out there in the bay, and that the generals here must pin their hopes on the possibility of a blunder on Washington's part that permits them to break free of this holding."

Missus James' needles never stopped flashing in and out of her work. "You've some experience in the movement of armies across a landscape. Will Washington arrive within a matter of days, a fortnight, months? I know that we cannot predict the outcome of the contest until it is joined, if even then, but can you hazard a guess as to when it might begin?"

Anna released him and turned toward the widow, and he shrugged.

"I would suppose that they are likelier to be here within a fortnight than a month," he speculated. "However, once they arrive, I cannot predict how long it might take before the fight breaks out. General Washington may opt to simply starve the British out of here, or force them into attempting a foolhardy assault over the fortifications. Or he may come in and start banging at their defenses straightaway."

Anna turned pale. "Might we truly be trapped within a lengthy siege, without any hope of supply from either the British or what American friends we still have in these parts?"

"Be still," Missus James snapped, before Nathaniel could even answer. "We have prepared ourselves for the possibility that we would be caught in the same trap that the British have set for themselves from the moment that the possibility became apparent. Although"—she fixed Nathaniel with a glare—"the potatoes will be quite difficult to enjoy without any fuel with which to cook them."

Nathaniel ducked his head in acknowledgment, answering, "In truth, I did not continue to search for firewood after I learned the news which I brought you in its stead. I shall go back out and see whether I may be granted permission to range out beyond the fortifications, or whether there are perhaps some remnants of the houses which have been pulled down in town which will answer."

Before he could leave, though, Anna had another thought, and she asked, "Is there not the possibility that the contest will be joined from the sea instead? Might not the French choose to sail down the river at any time?"

"Aye, that possibility exists, but I can tell you that I saw with my own eyes that the British are at this hour busily employed in destroying perhaps a dozen of their own ships for the sole purpose of providing a barrier to any enemy fleet that might think to approach from the bay. More than that, though, are the batteries that we have seen and commented on atop the bluffs."

Anna nodded as she remembered the stout fortifications thrown up seemingly overnight and apparently at every point along the top of the bluff that had a clear view of the water, and Nathaniel continued.

"As frightful a weight of iron as those French ships can throw, the cannon and howitzers in those batteries are not constrained by the same limitations of space or stability as apply to a ship. Too, they command the high ground, and no ship can even contemplate countering the advantage that provides."

He shook his head. "Nay, the French are exceedingly unlikely to try the river, as much as our guests may appear to fear that."

He thought for a moment, and then turned back to the widow James. "On reflection, having met General Lafayette, if only briefly, I suspect that if it were still his decision, he might well come in here with his guns blazing. He seems the sort to take what opportunities lay before him. For his part, General Washington seems more inclined to give his enemies the chance to retreat and give up their ill-gotten gains."

Shrugging, he added, "There is no retreat here, though, save into the river, and even the British are not so determined that they will fight to the last man. Time will tell, of course, and events may yet come to pass that will change the balance of the situation here, but on the whole, I think that I should rather be in General Washington's boots today than in Lord Cornwallis'."

Chapter 26

The tension in the air, transmitted almost as an infectious miasma from the British forces moving about the town, had everyone in the James' house on edge. It didn't help that they had tasted nothing but potatoes for days. Although Nathaniel had been able to bring in enough splintered lumber from the houses that had been pulled down, even the best of Anna's meager kitchen skills could only make the plain staple appealing.

In addition, they'd been reduced to drinking plain hot water, as there was no tea to be had anywhere, and what onions and hoarded suet they'd had at the beginning of the occupation were but wistful memories now.

Nathaniel could hear Anna and Missus James speaking in sharp tones in the kitchen. He walked to the doorway and leaned against the wall, hoping that their disagreement would not descend into a full-blown argument.

"Can you not visit your fine home and see what your cook put up there? Your brother would not begrudge you that, would he?" The older woman had been peevish for some time with the knowledge that Anna's house stood unmolested.

Anna replied, "Were my brother to discover me in my house, I do not doubt that he would turn me over to the British for their entertainment, so poisoned has his mind become against me in my betrothal. He told me nearly as much the last time I saw him on the street."

"Bring my cleaver with you, then, and he'll not give you nearly so much trouble, should he find you at all."

"Oh, that is just a marvelous idea. No, instead of one angry and sputtering brother to deal with, then we would have the wrath of the British army brought down on this house."

"Let them come!" The widow's voice had every bit of the fire that they had heard from her when they first met her. "They will learn that a determined old woman is nothing to be trifled with!" She mimed waving her poker through the air.

Nathaniel smiled at the memory of the day they'd met, and was about to make a comment to try to defuse the irritation that was evident in both women's faces, when the sharp sound of musket fire caused all of their heads to snap around in the direction from which the sound had come.

The reports of individual shots were joined then by the deeper boom of a cannon, and Nathaniel and the two women acted as one to start down the narrow stairs into the cellar.

As they descended into the darkness, Anna's voice came up from below Nathaniel on the stairs. "Do you think this is Lafayette's attack?"

Down in the cellar, the widow James had found the candles stored against this day. She struck a spark into the prepared charcloth and quickly lit a taper from the brief flare of flame it produced.

Now on firmer footing as he could see the stairs more clearly, Nathaniel finished coming down into the cellar and answered Anna.

"'Tis difficult to know yet. I only hear a few cannon firing, and if it were a general attack, I would expect to hear much more. In addition, there has been no indication yet that the American and allied forces have invested any works outside the redoubts our guests have erected, and even a surprise attack will likely require cannon to effect any substantial gains."

Another cannon shot boomed, though muffled by the house above them, as though to give punctuation to his comments. Just audible was the ongoing *crack* and *pop* of muskets, and Nathaniel even fancied that he could hear the shouts of men above the crack of gunpowder.

He made his way to a barrel standing on end and sat down heavily, memory overcoming him. The reek of burning gunpowder was sharp in his nose, and the groans of dying men sounded in his ears. The comforting smell of damp earth and dry timbers from the basement faded away, and all he could smell was the sharp metallic scent of his own blood as it flowed from his shattered arm to soak into the soil on which he lay.

His companions lay on either side of him, their death agonies written upon their faces, and the Redcoat who'd fallen along with them stared sightlessly at Nathaniel, his life's blood still leaking from between his stiffening fingers.

The *pop* and *boom* of distant gunfire faded to just a final few shots, and then fell silent. Nathaniel became aware that Anna was crouched down beside him where he lay on the packed dirt floor of the cellar. Her eyes were bright in the dim candlelight, reflecting tears that still hung at the edges of her eyelashes.

He was startled to realized that his own eyes were streaming, as well, and he released a deep, shuddering breath that almost seemed as though it had been raggedly drawn by someone else.

She spoke his name again, her voice quiet and her tone almost desperate.

He nodded slowly and took a more deliberate breath. "Yes, Anna. I'm sorry—the sound of the fight stirred the memories of my own battle, and they overcame me for a moment."

"You were screaming, Nathaniel, as though someone was chopping off your—oh," she said suddenly, her eyes dropping to where his stump was within his shirt, before she looked away, guilt etched on her features.

He sat up and reached out to brush the tip of his fingers across her cheek. His throat was raw enough that he had no difficulty believing that he had been making a terrible ruckus, and the fear and hurt on her face made his heart ache.

"It will be all right, Anna," he said quietly. "My ghosts will haunt me, but they will not master me. You have already convinced me that I am a whole man, even if I no longer possess a whole body. This"—he raised his stump—"does not take away what is important to me."

She did not turn to face him, looking instead at the timbers that reinforced the cellar wall across from where they sat. "I know that, Nathaniel," she said. "If anything, you seem to be more whole than someone like my brother, who retains his limbs but has lost his care for the family that he grew up in, and the country that made our station in life possible."

She brushed away her tears impatiently. "The hardship you have survived has marked you, though, and I am not speaking of your arm. Sometimes, when you think I do not notice, you look out to the horizon, as though you are scanning for enemy troops there, and when you hear a noise in the dark, you jerk as though you're afraid you will be shot again."

Anna finally turned to look into his eyes. "I know that we're not safe in this town, with the British thick on the ground about us, and our allies gathering with the intent to crush them and drive them out. But even when no threat is nearby, you are alert for any possible danger. It frightens me, Nathaniel. The amount of pain and fear that is locked in your mind is terrifying."

Nathaniel held her gaze as he thought over what she was saying. Finally, he closed his eyes for a moment and let his chin drop in acceptance before looking her in the eye again. "You have the right of it, Anna. I am always on the alert for dangers, even when none are present. I've told myself it is out of concern that you should never suffer the sort of loss that I have, but it is more than that."

He sighed. "Until the day comes when I sleep beneath a stone, I will bear the marks of my experience, and not just here"—he again raised his stump—"but here." He tapped the side of his head. "I cannot promise that you will never again see those ghosts torturing me, but I will give you my word that they will never bring you to grief."

"I believe that you will never mean to harm me in any way, but I cannot help but worry that when you have lost the use of your faculties in some fit as seized you just now . . ." She trailed off.

He reached out and took her hand in his own. "I will do whatever you need me to do in order to feel as though I am no danger to you, Anna. I truly do not believe that there is any risk that I might harm anyone else, or even myself when I am haunted, but if you are frightened of me, I will stay away from you." He gulped hard as he said it, but he looked into her eyes steadily.

"No, never that," she cried out and threw her arms around him. "I am promised to you, by my own will, and my feelings for you have not changed one whit. If anything, I am more committed to our friendship and our partnership than ever."

She pulled back, her hands on his shoulders. "I may fear for you, and even for myself, but I will not let mere fright stand in the way of our joy together." She seemed to come to a decision, and added, "Whatever your torments, we will face them together."

"Thank you, my dear friend," Nathaniel said, and gathered her into his embrace.

After a moment, Missus James spoke up from the far corner of the cellar. "If you two are finished, I should like to go back upstairs and learn whether our rescuers have prevailed, or whether we will continue to eat potatoes tonight."

Chapter 27

Anna and Nathaniel walked hand-in-hand down the road, taking advantage of an apparent lull in the skirmishes that had persisted since the initial outburst of violence between the massed armies. It was risky to be out and about, but it was maddening to sit in the house without news, and Anna had insisted that they take at least a brief walk. Nathaniel had agreed in the hopes that he might be able to learn something of the situation, as well.

All they could do indoors was await the next burst of cannon fire that would drive them into the cellar. Outdoors, they could at least try to get a sense of what was happening around them.

Nathaniel swept his hand over the landscape along the length of the British line.

"The Americans and their allies have set up all along in a line mirroring that behind which our English guests now cower, up to where the swamp about the creek makes movement impossible. Part of it is built around the fortifications that Cornwallis had his men burn to prevent them falling into our hands, but most of it is their own investment."

"Where did the fight we heard the other day take place, do you know?"

He pointed to a squat redoubt just visible over the line of earthworks that the British had erected. "That position there, which sits by itself, as I understand it, attracted the attention of a French company. The soldier I spoke to seemed quite boastful about the fact that the British let their enemies come quite close before opening fire on them."

Nathaniel shook his head sadly and shuddered. "He told me with great satisfaction how that little adventure cost the French some sixty men and a handful of officers, all killed near to where you and I used to walk together on a sunny summer's afternoon."

Anna looked grave and thoughtful before she replied, "That these men came all the way from France for the purpose of helping us gain our independence from the Crown, only to fall right here... it is difficult to make sense of."

His mood now somber to match hers, Nathaniel answered, "Their sacrifice must be honored and remembered, however this larger contest is decided." They walked on a few more paces, and he added, "As must be the losses suffered by so many in this war."

She squeezed his hand in understanding. The long rays of the setting sun were making them both squint, so they turned around to return to the widow James' house, their shadows long across the ground before them.

Looking out over the river, Nathaniel said idly, "I wish that the British would try fire ships against the French again."

Anna gave him a quizzical look, and he hastened to add, "Only because I want to see them for myself, not because I wish to have any harm come to our protectors from the Royal Navy here. It must have been quite a sight, watching a whole ship burn as it drifted down in the current, never mind three of them at once."

He smirked. "What fools the British must have felt, though, when the French slipped their anchors and moved aside, only to watch the fire ships run aground on the bar out there, harmlessly burning to the water. Seeing the British waste their efforts so seems like capital entertainment to me."

A sudden, distant crackle of gunfire hardly turned their heads, so common had it become.

Listening carefully, Nathaniel nodded in the direction of Gloucester. "It's all the way on the other side of the river."

Peering toward the shadowed water of the river, he noticed a mass floating near the shore and pointed. "What on earth is that?"

Anna peered at where he was indicating, and examined the spot with her sharper eyes. She gasped. "It's their horses," she said sadly. "Good heavens, the British have killed their horses and thrown them into the river."

Nathaniel shook his head. "Truly, things are at a terrible pass, then, if they are resorting to such measures. 'Tis true that there is no forage remaining within the walls of the fortifications that they have built, and they cannot just turn the poor beasts free to become tools of the Americans' attack, but they must have little faith that they will fight free of this place if they are destroying their horses."

The sporadic pops of musketry subsided, but Nathaniel was still thinking of the danger that they were needlessly exposing themselves to, so he guided their steps back toward the house.

"We should not have come outside, even when things seem quiet," he said. "The very nature of a siege is that it is precisely when things seem quiet that they may turn quite active indeed."

Anna leaned into him, and she did not resist his pull toward the widow's house. "Thank you for humoring me, Nathaniel."

Her voice was quiet and sad as she continued, "Those poor horses, caught up in a war they had nothing to do with."

He answered, "Aye, 'tis a bad time for any creature that is caught in the middle between these two armies. But then, no war is easy on the innocent bystanders, never mind the participants."

Chapter 28

It seemed that the sun had scarcely risen when the great guns began to speak—though from which side, Nathaniel could not tell. He rose from his bed and pulled on his clothing quickly, meeting Anna and Missus James in the kitchen. Wearily, without a word, all three of them descended the stairs into the basement. The older woman paused to light a taper at the morning's fire in the hearth, just set, and then swept her poker over it, scattering the wood in an attempt to save some of it for later.

When Nathaniel had first proposed that they prepare to retreat with their few remaining neighbors to the relative safety of the portion of the lower town that the British now permitted them, somewhat shielded from American fire by the bluff, Missus James had been resistant.

"I did not permit the British to chase me out of my home, and I cannot see how I should let our own forces do what the enemy could not."

"I do not fear that our armies would come to the door and threaten violence," Nathaniel explained, "but a cannon ball or a musket shot would not need to be aimed at us to strike the house— and it would go through these walls as readily as they do flesh and bone."

He held up the stump of his arm for emphasis, adding, "Nobody else in this house needs to suffer what I have in the name of stubborn pride. If you will not leave this house, then perhaps we can make the cellar comfortable enough."

She harrumphed, but the mention of cannon shot seemed to have gotten her attention.

They'd spent a few days filling and carrying casks of water into the cellar, and of course, the potatoes were stored down there in normal times, anyway. Pallets for sleeping, should the need arise to spend the night, and candles and a few other creature comforts completed their preparations.

Although the sound of musket or rifle fire had been enough to send them down the stairs at first, now it was only the big guns that they truly feared. Of course, any gunfire in nearby streets would have been cause for immediate action, but a mortar shot that started out aimed at the British line could easily overshoot and fill the air overhead with deadly shards of iron, and a cannon ball might skip and bounce along the ground, straight into the wall of the house. A smaller ball simply had more obstacles to pass through between them and the line, and did not pose a realistic threat.

This morning, though, it was the big guns that were playing upon the line.

Sitting on his familiar cask, wishing that they'd had time to heat water before the fighting had started, Nathaniel yawned, and the widow James nodded at him knowingly.

"You could go back to sleep, if you can sleep through the din," she said.

"Nay, there's no chance that I could sleep through that, and if I could, it would be an open invitation for the old specters to come and haunt me. No, I will stay awake, and contemplate the errors of my ways." He flashed a smile, and Anna chuckled.

"That will not occupy you for long," she said.

"If you cannot remember enough errors to distract you until the guns are still, I will be glad to help," Missus James interjected, and all three of them laughed.

However, the guns continued to bark and boom throughout the day. Any time they thought that whatever was happening above might have ended, a fresh round of firing would start up. More than once, the widow already had her foot on the stairs to go back up to the kitchen when the shooting sounded again.

Finally, she huffed and continued up the stairs, even as the guns spoke. She tossed over her shoulder, "The hearth will protect me anyway, and we've got to have cooked food and hot water if we're to keep spirit and flesh together."

Nathaniel pursed his mouth, but did not argue the point. His belly was growling, and her observation was likely true anyway. Even a ball that went straight through the wood of the walls would be stopped by the solid stone of the hearth.

From the pallet where she had laid down, Anna asked, "What do you imagine is the cause of so much firing?"

Nathaniel shrugged. "I do not think that it is our artillery firing on our guests, else we should have heard some balls striking nearby, as someone's shot went long, or bounced off something at its target. Given that, it seems likely that the British are trying to dissuade our men as they approach the walls here, or otherwise endanger the fortifications."

He looked thoughtful and then added, "Had it only lasted for a short while, I might have thought that it was an attempt to break through the siege and find some relief in the countryside, or that some unsuspected British force had come to the reinforcement of this place from behind the American lines, and was trying to make its way into the town."

He gestured at the candle guttering in its last half-inch. "We've been down here long enough that we ought start another candle, though, so that seems unlikely."

Another boom sounded, and Anna flinched visibly. "Won't they run out of powder and shot eventually, if they continue firing so regularly?"

"Aye, I would think so, particularly without any new supply possible by sea or land." He shrugged. "It may be that they laid in a greater supply than they needed of those, while neglecting to provide for the men who would need to serve the guns."

"Or the horses needed to pull them."

"Sure. I've seen similar messes during the course of my own service. As many shirts as would clothe a regiment, but no more shoes than would supply a small company." He made a wry face. "Or it may be that they have decided that the expenditure of powder and ball is in the service of a worthy enough goal to impoverish themselves of the same at a later point in the fight."

The guns spoke again, and Nathaniel shook his head. "Whatever they hope to accomplish with this, I would surely like to see them either meet or abandon their goal. This is no way to spend a day."

Anna arose from her pallet and lit a fresh taper from the last bit of the first one. "Well, you did say that the two forces would strike sparks where they met."

"That I did." Another report punctuated his comment, and he added wryly, "I only wish that they could be somewhat less noisy in doing so."

Missus James came down the stairs now, grunting over a cooking kettle held out far enough to avoid burning herself on it. Nathaniel rose and went up the stairs to take it from her, but Anna *tsk*ed at him and stepped in front of him to take it.

"Boiled potatoes enough to last us until tomorrow, if need be," the older woman commented, and turned to go back up the stairs. "I'll go and get the hot water."

Anna set the kettle down on one of the upended casks, and Nathaniel peered inside. The smell of the cooked potatoes made his mouth water, and Anna stood beside him, her arm warm against his.

"I hadn't known how hungry I was until this very moment," she said, and he nodded in silent but fervent agreement.

Missus James came back down the stairs, and set the water kettle on the floor next to the cask that Nathaniel had pressed into service as a makeshift table. "Want to bring another barrel over for this?"

He sprang to follow her suggestion, and she produced three heavy plates and three knives from the oversized pockets in her apron, handing them to Anna. "Had to carry that carefully to be sure that the thing didn't hit the plates and crack them," she said, indicating the water kettle with a tilt of her head. "Here, take these, and I'll go fetch our cups, as it seems we're to be here a bit longer."

Nathaniel finished setting the second cask beside the first, and lifted the kettle up onto it. Anna set the plates and knives beside the kettle and took one of each for herself. She stuck the point of her knife into a potato in the larger cooking kettle and transferred it to her plate. Nathaniel brought a set of smaller casks to set around the larger barrels to use as seats.

"No reason we can't be civilized," he said, setting the last of them behind Anna for her to settle onto.

The widow James came back down the stairs and nodded approvingly at the arrangement.

"Quite civilized indeed," she said. "Let us break our fast." She smiled over at Anna, who was already sucking in her breath to cool her first bite of potato, and added, "Those who haven't already, that is."

Chapter 29

Other than brief trips upstairs to help Missus James at the hearth, or to empty chamber pots out the back door, it had been nearly a fortnight since any of them had seen daylight. Though the firing was not as constant as it had been on the first day, iron and lead were now flying in both directions, without much in the way of warning at all.

While at the hearth, Missus James reported that she had witnessed a wagon bearing a pile of enemy dead stop before a house whose cellar opened to the outside, and the corpses were being carried down into the abandoned house's cellar.

It was enough to almost make Nathaniel glad that his ma's house had not survived the reinforcement of the British lines.

He commented to Anna, "A pulled-down house can be rebuilt at some expense and difficulty at the end of this affair. One that has been used as a grave for a dozen men or more, though? Is there any way to recover such a property to a mundane use?"

Anna shuddered delicately, and though Nathaniel could not see her—the last of the widow James' hoarded tapers had guttered into darkness days before—he could guess that her face was white at the thought.

"It is almost enough to make me hope that my brother still holds our house, that it will not be put to such a low use. Is there any inch of this town that will not have received blood at the end of this contest, though, be it British blood or our own? It hardly seems possible that anyone could live here again after all that has happened."

The crashing sound of a cannon ball striking the neighboring house seemed to underscore her question. So far, only one had struck Missus James' house, passing through the roof and leaving a hole that now admitted rain through the widow's bedroom and down into the entrance hall whenever it stormed. Still, when he chanced peeks past the shutters at the houses nearby that were visible, Nathaniel thought others on the surrounding streets had suffered far worse.

Nathaniel gathered Anna in with his arm and held her, stroking her hair with his hand. "I do not know, my dear friend. There has been so much destruction across the countryside that it is hard to see how life anywhere in this country could possibly return to normal, if the war were to end this very day."

He listened to the seemingly endless crash and crackle of gunfire outside and said, "And even that seems like an impossible dream. There is too much animosity between our two nations at this point for either to give any ground. Either we win our total independence and have no more involvement again with kings and parliaments, or they crush our revolt utterly, and erase the idea of men being ruled only by their own consent for all time."

He shook his head. "There does not seem to be any space between these two positions for a compromise anymore. There was a time, when this affair started, that I heard my pa say that the whole thing would be over in a day, if Parliament would but grant us the representation we were due by our numbers."

Anna said, "Do you really think so?"

He shrugged. "I don't know enough to have an opinion about the matter. I know only what my father's feelings were at that time. I misdoubt that he would take the same position today, with all that this war has now cost us."

After a thoughtful moment, he added, "Nor do I believe that the British government could convince their people to accept such a settlement, with all of the blood we have spilled, and the destruction of so much of value to them."

"So, we fight?"

"We fight, until one or the other of us is destroyed." Listening to the din outside, he said, "Or both."

From her pallet in the corner of the basement, Missus James said, "My money's still on our boys. These occupiers have expended hundreds of men and God alone knows how many barrels of powder and shot in this place alone, only to find themselves with no way to escape it."

Nathaniel could hear her shifting to find a more comfortable position before she continued, "Yesterday, as I was preparing water, I heard two soldiers speaking outside the shutters to the kitchen as they hid from their duty for a moment's rest. They were greatly depressed at the state of affairs in their camp, and they were both remarking on how little hope there is of any relief, and how close they are to defeat if there can be none."

Nathaniel had to guess that she shrugged in the darkness then, before she went on.

"They complained that their rations were reduced to the point of slow starvation, and that they had been forced to slaughter their horses some weeks ago, as those unfortunate beasts had nothing left to eat, either."

"Oh, we saw them," Anna said. "They tossed the poor things into the river."

"Aye," said the older woman, "And the men I heard were full of regret at the loss of the meat now."

Anna gasped, "What a horrible, wicked thing for them to say!"

The widow gave a harsh bark of laughter. "Wicked or not, an army depends upon having full stomachs to maintain its strength, whether for fighting or for fleeing. With their rations so desperately depleted, I should be surprised if our precious Lord Cornwallis can hold out for another fortnight—and I would be less surprised if he should call for terms with Washington this very day."

Chapter 30

The firing had ceased. It had been an hour or more since the guns had gone silent on all sides, and Nathaniel and the two women had emerged into the kitchen, peering out through the gap between the shutters to see what they could learn about what was happening without.

"I see nobody at all," Anna said quietly, though the sound of her voice seemed to echo in the quiet house.

Missus James replied in an equally soft voice, "That's not unusual. The entire time we were below, I saw soldiers on only a few occasions. They are mostly at the earthworks, or in their encampments behind the line."

The quiet of the house and the still town outside was almost eerie after a fortnight and more of nearly constant cannon and musket fire from one quarter or another. There had been lulls, of course, particularly at night, but most mornings, they had not missed a rooster's crow to wake them, as it had been replaced by the cough and sputter of the guns.

This morning's substitute for the cock's crow had been particularly rousing, and Nathaniel had jerked awake from a dream that yet again brought him face-to-face with his dying friends and enemies. He had grown inured to these nightmares, though, as the sound of mortars and cannon in the dark of the cellar was almost so familiar as to have become comfortable.

This break in the gunfire, however, had already lasted long enough that Nathaniel was daring to hope that it would not resume. And that, of course, could only have happened if the British had finally capitulated. Had they been reinforced somehow, there would have been even more furious fire, and the quiet now would be punctuated by audible huzzahs and celebrations.

None of that could be heard, though, and Nathaniel was curious enough to find out what he could that he said to Anna and Missus James, "Stay here. I'm going to go upstairs and see what I can from up there." The older woman pursed her lips at being given orders in her own house, but Anna just nodded, her eyes wide.

Nathaniel mounted the stairs quietly, as though the squeak of a riser might bring a return of the fighting outside. When he reached the hallway, he turned into the widow's room first, both to look out toward the British line through her window, and to assess how much damage had been done by the ball that had crashed through.

Boards hung down loosely from the gaping hole in the ceiling, and the cannon ball itself lay inert where it had rolled to the corner of the room. A puddle of water still stood under the hole, left from the hard rain that had pounded the town the prior evening. The smell of decay was heavy in the air, and mold was visible on the hand-knotted rug that peeked out from under the widow James' bed.

Sighing at the damage, Nathaniel made his way to the window, where one of the shutters had been jarred open by the impact. Careful to approach the open window in such a way that he would be difficult to spot from below, he peered out into the afternoon light.

He could just see the top of the British barricades over the neighboring house, and he was shocked to see just how thoroughly torn asunder they were. Not a single gun was visible in working order, though he could see the toppled and smashed remnants of several cannon and mortar sticking out of the jumbled mass of soil and wood that made up the British line.

On the far side of the barricade, he could see the line of the Americans and their allies' encampments on the hills behind town, well out of reach of the British artillery. Closer in, the spiked edges of defensive walls of trenches were just visible, and wisps of smoke from behind those gave him a definite sense that the trenches were well-manned and heavily armed.

Beyond the barricade, he could see the figure of a man hurrying back from the American line. As he drew closer to the British barricades, Nathaniel could see that he was an officer by a glint of the sun from his epaulettes.

The man had just disappeared from view when the American line opened up again, gouts of flame reaching out toward the town as cannon and mortars fired, and the incredible din of what seemed like every musket on the entire line firing at once.

Nathaniel ducked down and hurried out of the room, marveling as he did at the visible ripples in the pool of water on the floor, as it was disturbed by the unbelievable noise from outside.

He rushed down the stairs and into the kitchen, where the women were already in the process of going down into the cellar. Following them, he called out, "It looked as though our guests called for a parley, but the talks failed, and as soon as their negotiator returned to their lines, the Americans resumed their attack."

Anna called over her shoulder, nearly shouting to be heard,

"I had such hopes that it was over, too."

"Lord Cornwallis likely failed again to accord proper respect to the armies of General Washington," Missus James said tartly when they were all back in the cellar. In the dim light admitted by the open door above them, Nathaniel could see her tight smile.

"Or perhaps his Excellency the General has concluded that it is advantageous to further persuade Lord Cornwallis that he is well and truly defeated," Nathaniel answered, smiling more gaily. "In any event, I am convinced on the basis of what I could see that the end of this affair is quite near indeed. There is little remaining of the British defenses of their stronghold here, and the act of sending an envoy under a flag over to parley is a plain acknowledgment of their state."

Anna sat heavily on a cask well-worn now from such usage. "I fervently hope that you are right in this, Nathaniel. This ordeal has been terrible, and its termination is much to be anticipated." She smiled up at him. "Not all of our time here has been terrible, of course, but I am ready to walk in the sunlight with you again, rather than huddle here in the darkness."

"I should like that myself, of all things," Nathaniel smiled into the low light.

The widow huffed and settled down on her pallet. "I'll be trying to sleep, while you two lovebirds go on sighing and gawping at each other. 'Tis tiresome for a lonely old woman to hear, day in and day out for so long, don't you know?"

Although Missus James had made such comments at many occasions throughout their confinement in the cellar, Nathaniel had more than once caught her smiling to herself as she looked at them talking together, Anna's head close by his that they might speak quietly enough for some semblance of privacy.

Though such proximity for so long a time might have unmasked any number of flaws in some people, Nathaniel felt that he had only come to know Anna's finer qualities throughout the past fortnight. They had talked about every topic imaginable, and had laid plans for their future together, complete with alternatives for achieving what they hoped under either British rule or American government.

Of late, their talks had turned to such considerations as what kind of house they might need to build for themselves, and how Nathaniel might establish himself in some business once the British were gone, at least from their town.

As the afternoon stretched into night, the guns outside stopping again, and then starting, then falling silent, Nathaniel came around to this question again. "I cannot presume that my father will be able to recover his prior position, nor support me in any fashion, as it seems likely that all of his holdings have been reduced under the occupation."

"There is always opportunity for a man who has so quickly taken to the keeping of books as you have."

"I will still need to learn my letters fully to be of any use to most men," he answered, "but I will agree that I should be able to find some position that will enable me to support you, once I have done so."

"I am not certain that I wish to wait that long, my dear friend, before I am joined to you." Nathaniel could hear the smile in her voice as she spoke. "Surely, my father will have some means remaining that we may rely upon as you are getting yourself established."

"If that is the case, then I should like more than anything to be married at our first opportunity."

An explosion sounded at that moment, the sharp concussion followed in a few moments by the sound of shards showering into the roof overhead.

He sighed. "That will require more repairs after the end of this."

"There will be much that needs to be repaired when this is over," Anna replied. "I am most gratified, however, at what we have constructed anew in the midst of all of this destruction." She shifted then, bringing her lips to Nathaniel's cheek. "Good night, my dear friend, and let us face the morning in the hopes that quiet and peace can be established for good."

Chapter 31

Quiet, indeed, did establish itself overnight, and it continued into the following morning. Nathaniel was hardly able to contain himself, so great was his need to know what was transpiring without.

Returning to his post at the widow's bedroom window at dawn, he saw, to his amazement, the British forces crowding the top of their ramparts in a ragged mass, staring out over the torn earth at their opponents. For their part, the American and allied forces stood at the top of their own earthworks, gazing back just as quietly.

The guns were silent, and no muskets were shouldered to menace either side. There were just men in their hundreds, perhaps even thousands, looking at one another in quiet contemplation of the horror that they had together created and endured. From where he stood, Nathaniel could see that the soldiers on the close side of the muddy divide stood with their shoulders drooping, their bearing radiating weariness and dejection.

This sight, beyond anything else he'd seen or heard, convinced Nathaniel that the battle was truly at an end.

Moving to the other side of the house, he looked out over the river, where an even more surprising sight greeted him. Of the great British fleet of transports and warships, nothing remained but a virtual forest of masts and a great array of half-burned wreckage.

"My God," he said almost involuntarily under his breath to himself.

There would be no retreat, no escape for Cornwallis' great army, only surrender under terms that must even at this moment be under negotiation.

He returned to the cellar, where Anna and Missus James were still lying on their pallets. "I think," he said without preamble, "that we may safely repair to our own beds. It appears that the affair is all over but the ceremony. The British have lost the siege."

Anna leapt up from her pallet and threw her arms around Nathaniel, and he was surprised to find himself weeping along with her, so great was the sense of relief. He was even more surprised when the widow James joined in their embrace, wrapping her arms around them both.

After a long time, he raised his head from Anna's shoulder and turned to the older woman. "We owe you our lives," he said. "When I was hurt, you could have refused us a safe haven and left us to the unlikely mercy of the British army's doctors. When the battle began in earnest, you could have turned us out to seek shelter with the rest of the townspeople below the bluff. Instead, you welcomed us into your cellar with you."

"Oh, stop, you," she replied. "Without you having stumbled into my house, I would have had no food grown to sustain myself, and would have had to throw myself at the mercy of our occupiers. I needed you as much as you needed me, and I'll hear no more about it."

She released the young couple from her embrace, and bent to gather up their dishes. "Bring up the kettles, would you? We'll need to come back down for the bedding. I've looked at my room, and I'll have to sleep in the kitchen until I can get that mess cleaned up."

"Oh, what stuff," Anna exclaimed. "You'll sleep in the bed you were so kind as to lend to me. I'll bring my pallet up to Nathaniel's room and sleep on the floor there. I doubt that I could get any decent rest without the sound of his snoring anyway."

Missus James favored the girl with a skeptical look but said nothing. Nathaniel didn't know whether to be offended or complimented that Anna wanted to stay near him. For her part, Anna gave a merry giggle, the first such that Nathaniel had heard in weeks. He settled on shooting her an answering smile, and then gathered up the handles of the two empty kettles to carry them upstairs.

"Set the kettles by the hearth," Missus James said, "and then go and gather the bedding. I shall be happy enough to see that cellar never used for anything but a storeroom for supplies and root crops again."

"Aye," agreed Nathaniel.

He brought Anna's pallet up and set it far enough away from his bed that there should be no hint of impropriety in the arrangement, but close enough that they could talk in the night, if they wished.

Once they'd removed their effects to the second floor, Nathaniel and Anna followed Missus James to the doorway of her bedroom, where she stood for a moment at the threshold, looking at the mess and shaking her head. She stepped into the room to go up to the window, where she gazed out at the same scene that had greeted Nathaniel.

As he and Anna joined her at the window, it didn't look to

him as though anything had changed. The men on the smashed British earthworks milled about a bit now, but their bearing had not changed a whit.

He realized with a jolt that this must have been how he looked, walking across South-Carolina, his stump still aching in its limp and empty sleeve, and his heart aching nearly as much. He felt a moment of compassion for the enemy soldiers, tempered by the tremendous wreckage visible all about them, the remains of his once-idyllic, small town.

Uninvited and unwanted, they had brought this destruction here by their presence. Gazing out at the punctured rooftops and shattered windows of the neighboring houses, he pursed his lips and shook his head to dispel any growing impulse to find anything in common with the British and Loyalist forces.

Their cases were in no way parallel to his own, he forced himself to acknowledge. Most of them had come from across the ocean to re-impose the capricious and cruel will of the unanswerable Parliament and the Crown itself on the colonies, while he had sought to defend neighbors and friends from that fate.

His cause was just; theirs was mercenary. He fought for the high ideas of liberty and equality, while they fought for the exercise of naked power. His was the side of the angels, after all, for why else would God have permitted their side to be laid low here, in this place, before his very eyes?

And then he remembered the soldier of the green, green grass of home, and the mother and sisters and sweetheart—the man who had, in his dying breath, leveled the accusation that Nathaniel's ball had been the one that had ended his life.

Nathaniel remembered, then, how he'd prepared for the

battle, loaded his musket, and pressed the lead ball to his lips for luck before dropping it into the barrel of his gun and ramming it home. The next mortal flesh that ball had touched had been that of the British soldier, and Nathaniel could not be certain that anything he had fought for had been worth that price.

He stepped back from the window, then, and Anna noticed that his manner had changed.

"What is the matter, Nathaniel?"

He shook his head and replied, "It's nothing that I can easily explain, but I find myself wondering what we have accomplished, what good have we done, when I see how much devastation has been wrought in both property and men."

Missus James said curtly, "We've won our independence from the King, that's what. Unless he should like to send another army the size of Lord Cornwallis' for us to reduce in like manner, it will be difficult for His Majesty to prevail anywhere in this country."

She bent and pulled the moldy rug from under her bed. "I've a lot of cleaning to do in here, to prepare for whatever workmen I can find, so that they can repair the roof in here and stop the weather from finishing what our friends on the American line have started. Help or get out of the way, but stop brooding at the window."

Chapter 32

The British were gone from the town, save for those whose corpses that had not yet been hauled out of cellars and brought to some hasty but decent burial elsewhere. Nathaniel and Anna wandered throughout the desolation of the roads of York-Town, silent and holding hands for comfort.

The end of the siege had not seemed real as they'd watched the occupiers march out onto the field outside of their earthworks, their flags wrapped in shame and dishonor, their drums somber, to stack their arms in great piles. It had not felt like actual events unfolding as Nathaniel had stood quietly beside Anna and Missus James, and watched the deserters who'd come over to the British—including Anna's brother—board the ship bound for New York to avoid General Washington's promised dance upon the gallows.

Even seeing Washington's great army gather up its own armaments and those they had captured to go on to seek their next engagement in this endless war had a sense of unreality to it. The last of the wagons pulling away behind its straining team, bumping and swaying down the rutted road until it disappeared over the crest of the ridge, had looked like a specter, rather than history marching onward.

Nathaniel and Anna were coming back up from the lower town, walking side-by-side on the road that still cut through the bluff, largely unchanged but for deeper the ruts dug by wagons and cannon alike by all that had happened around it. On the road ahead, they saw the figures of the first people returning home from whatever refuge they'd found while the siege ran its bloody course.

A pair of the returnees split away from the rest and ran forward.

Nathaniel strained to see who they were, and then remarked to Anna wonderingly, "Is that my ma . . . and my pa? Together?"

A moment later, his parents arrived, breathless, and gathered up both Anna and Nathaniel in a joint embrace. Too overcome for words at first, his pa kept reaching up and stroking the side of Nathaniel's face, as though he could not believe that he was feeling it.

His ma was hardly any more coherent, but it was she who managed the first words that Nathaniel could make out among their sobs.

"We thought for certain that you'd been lost," she said. "We thought we'd lost you forever."

She buried her head in his shoulder, overcome again.

Nathaniel reached around his pa's shoulder to grip her arm in reassurance that he was really there. "We survived, Ma. I don't know quite how, but we survived."

His pa took a deep breath, regaining his composure enough to speak at last. "You cannot imagine what it was like, being forced to leave you behind, and then hearing only reports of total destruction here. We never expected to see you again in this life, son."

He looked over at Nathaniel's ma, who nodded in agreement. He continued, "We thought that we'd lost the only thing we've always agreed was the best of us both. Whatever future awaits us, we wanted only to share it with you. Thank God we will have the opportunity to do so."

With that, he put his arm around Nathaniel's ma, and pulled Nathaniel and Anna close, and there they stood for a long, long time.

Also in Audiobook

Many readers love the experience of turning the pages in a paper book such as the one you hold in your hands. Others enjoy hearing a skilled narrator tell them a story, bringing the words on the page to life.

Brief Candle Press has arranged to have *The Siege* produced as a high-quality audiobook, and you can listen to a sample and learn where to purchase it in that form by scanning the QR code below with your phone, tablet, or other device, or going to the Web address shown.

Happy listening!

bit.ly/TheSiegeAudio

Historical Notes

The Siege of Yorktown is one of those events where we have an embarrassment of riches when it comes to first-hand accounts and many other rich and detailed sources to draw on. I have made heavy use of the journal kept by the German officer Johann Ewald, as his account is both riveting and written from the perspective of someone deeply involved in the action leading up to Cornwallis' defeat. A few of the other events that I mention in the course of the story are particularly noteworthy, as well.

The account given by Jacob of Braddock's Defeat during the French and Indian War is my rendition of how it might have appeared to a soldier of the Virginia Militia. One part that I did not have to imagine was the very high regard in which Washington was held as a result of taking charge of extracting his army's overcome forces. Although he was not technically in the line of command, he took over for the mortally wounded General Braddock, leading the British forces away and avoiding their complete destruction or capture.

Curiously, both sides lost their commanders in a chaotic melee that was less a set battle than a tangled fight for survival. However, despite being greatly outnumbered, the French army's Indian allies and Canadien militia were better suited by training and temperament to turn the day to their advantage.

Yonahequah was a name that I encountered in researching

the interactions of the Cherokee with the American and British forces during the Revolution. He appears in the historical record as a Cherokee chief and signatory to a treaty long after the end of the Revolution. While I did not find any other mention of him in the historical record, it made sense to me that he must have been a young man in 1780, and perhaps the same qualities that brought him to a leadership role later in his life might have made him willing to let a maimed American soldier go unmolested.

The decline of Williamsburg after the capital of Virginia was moved to Richmond in the spring of 1780 was described by contemporary accounts as being at least as sudden and shocking to its residents as I've depicted it. Indeed, the town did not begin to recover until it reinvented itself in the 1920s as a modern-day interpretation of an 18th-century town. The reenactors there take their jobs very seriously, and the researchers and historians who support them have produced a wide variety of resources to improve the authenticity of the experience for their visitors.

The destruction of Richmond at the hands of Benedict Arnold was a stroke that was felt keenly throughout the new nation. For a capital city of one of its largest colonies to be put to the torch was, in some ways, a greater blow to morale than the disastrous capture of the city of Charleston the prior year. For those who had suffered through so many long years of open warfare already, it must have felt like defeat at the hands of the British was becoming inevitable.

Lafayette's visit to Yorktown before the British arrival there, and Cornwallis' scouting of the town both apparently occurred much as I've depicted them. It is intriguing that they both visited the town where they would meet in the culminating confrontation of the American Revolution, within mere weeks of one another. I am indebted to Steph Dray, who has just released a magnificent novel on Lafayette, for her advice on portraying him faithfully.

I chose to depict de Grasse's French fleet on its arrival to Chesapeake Bay being visible from the second floor of a residence in the upper part of York-Town for dramatic purposes. As far as I can reconstruct, it might have been theoretically visible from the steeple of the church, but it was probably not easily visible from the vantage where I've depicted it. Too, the sound of cannon as the French fleet engaged the British at the entrance of Chesapeake Bay may not have carried as far as York-Town. There is a report, though, of the sound of later confrontations at the mouth of the Chesapeake reaching listeners there, so perhaps this is not as free an invention as I might have feared.

The smoke of that exchange was reported as being visible from Gloucester (on the opposite shore of the York River) by Ewald in his invaluable journal of the campaign. He is silent on the question of whether this action was audible from his position, but he mentions that a later naval action in a similar position was, so I thought that this was a reasonable extrapolation.

Ewald speaks of foraging timber from plantations in the area to use in constructing the defenses at York-Town. It's pretty reasonable to expect that the houses in town would have been seen as another potential source of lumber, but the detail of preferentially tearing down the houses of patriots in the town itself is my own invention, based on the other sorts of abuses that the two sides heaped upon partisans of their opposition throughout the war.

Acknowledgements

I am greatly indebted to the dedicated historians and curators who preserve and interpret the history of major events in history, particularly when there is a specific geographical location where that history took place.

The material prepared and made available by the staffs of the incomparable Museum of the American Revolution in Philadelphia, and the American Revolution Museum at Yorktown helped me tremendously in developing my understanding of the experience of those who endured the siege at Yorktown.

My editor, Jen McDonnell, helped me to ensure that my writing was as crisp and clear as possible, as well as catching the inevitable typos that occur when one is writing late into the night. Any errors I introduced after her edits are wholly my own fault, of course.

Thank You

I deeply appreciate you spending the past couple of hundred pages with the characters and events of a world long past, yet hopefully relevant today.

If you enjoyed this book, I'd also be grateful for a kind review on your favorite bookseller's Web site or social media outlet. Word of mouth is the best way to make me successful, so that I can bring you even more high-quality stories of bygone times.

I'd love to hear directly from you, too—feel free to reach out to me via my Facebook page, Twitter feed, or Web site and let me know what you liked, and what you would like me to work on more.

Again, thank you for reading, for telling your friends about this book, for giving it as a gift or dropping off a copy in your favorite classroom or library. With your support and encouragement, we'll find even more times and places to explore together.

larsdhhedbor.com
Facebook: Lars.D.H.Hedbor
@LarsDHHedbor on Twitter

Enjoy a preview of the next book in the
Tales From a Revolution series:

The Fight

The sun beat down, as merciless as the flies that buzzed about, and all I could think about was death. Before me lay the heaped earth and dark grave of the father I'd scarcely gotten to know, taken in the summer of his forty-first year.

I was here out of a sense of despairing duty, having suffered the most painful blow this man could have devised to strike at me from beyond the grave he now occupied. It had begun with a sharp rap at the door of the mean little house that my mother and I occupied.

Mother was in one of her fits of despondency, and so when the knock came at the door, I was the one to answer it. A stranger stood in the bright sun, his hat held respectfully over his chest.

He looked me over and asked, "John Melcher?"

I nodded cautiously. "Aye, that's me."

He bowed ever so slightly, producing a folded and sealed paper and handing it to me. He straightened and stood, looking expectantly at me, so I slid my finger under the seal, dislodging the wax, and opened the paper.

I scanned it, my brow furrowing unconsciously as I made out the words written on it. "The presence of John Jacob Melcher or his duly appointed legal representative is requested at the reading of the last will of Colonel Isaac Melcher, late of Graeme Park, deceased this Wednesday last, 10th July instant. If no representative can be arranged, his undersigned executors messrs. Clifton, Eppele, and Lawersveyler will make the necessary arrangements to convey any bequest to you in as timely fashion as shall be practical. We are, yr. obedient &c."

Gone? Dead? The Colonel, the Barracks Master General, the dashing military officer, land speculator, the sharp-dealing cloth merchant, the distant father and flawed husband that my mother and I had known for all of my fourteen years on the planet, departed forever from this existence?

It was too much to take in, and I looked up from the page to see the stranger still looking at me. I asked, dumbly, "Is there something you need of me?"

"I was instructed to await your reading of this letter, and to learn whether you could accompany me back to the offices of the scrivener Baker for the reading."

Still dazed, I said, "Aye, of course. I shall need to gather my hat and inform my mother of my departure." He bowed again in acknowledgment, and I turned, leaving him standing in the doorway, outlined by the daylight without.

I stopped at the threshold of Mother's room, where she sat silently, her hands busily knotting and looping some lacework, her eyes staring blankly at the wall before her. She slowly took note of my presence, and her hands came to a stop as she looked up at me.

"The Colonel is dead," I said, seeking no soft words to cushion the hard fact.

She looked away from me abruptly and chewed her lip, silent tears springing to her eyes and trickling down her sunken cheeks. She closed her eyes, and I could see her shoulders shake as her hands fell limp over the piecework in her lap.

"I am summoned to hear his bequests. Do you need anything before I go?"

She shook her head, neither saying anything nor even looking at me. When she was feeling low, she might not speak to me for days at a stretch, or she might screech at me like one of the harpies in the Greek stories that the schoolmaster insisted I read. This time around, it had been silence, and even the news of her erstwhile husband's death was not enough to pierce that veil.

Look for The Fight: Tales From a Revolution - Pennsylvania _at your favorite booksellers._